CON

MW01114458

BY

PETER C. BRADBURY

Sometimes, you have to pay the Consequences of your actions.

Dedicated to my grandson Bryce, and the millions of other sufferers at the hands of bullies.

CHAPTER 1

James had been festering for years, building his list, and preparing himself physically and mentally for all the wrongs done to him during his thirty years. He was ready now to exact his revenge. Turn the tables on them all, and if they didn't apologize, then he would ensure they would never think about doing it again. To anybody.

His whole school life he felt he'd been bullied, ridiculed, and shunned. It had been mostly okay in class if the teacher was there, but at all other times he was chased, hit, picked on, or thrown at. James would have preferred to have been home schooled, but his mother was single and had to work while his estranged father rarely saw him. When he did, he just told James to fight back.

The only trouble was that he was a frail kid with bad eyes and spotty skin, and his mother kept his hair close to the scalp after he got hair lice once at Elementary School. She would never let him grow it out. James wasn't strong enough to play sports, his poor eyesight didn't help, even though he would have liked to play. So he stuck to studying and trying to keep out of everyone's way.

James and his mother lived in an old farmhouse with no neighboring kids for him to play with, but at least he'd been able to have pets. He preferred their company as they never judged him on his looks or weaknesses. They were as unconditional as his mother with their love.

One of the animals was wild and he called him Johnny. He thought Johnny Deer had a good ring to it. Johnny, along with his mother and siblings, would wander around the farmhouse, and for some reason Johnny took a liking to James. He would let James pet him from an early age, to even when he'd grown and his antlers got in the way. He was a very handsome buck and James loved to watch him run and graze.

Then Tommy Hilditch came with his gun.

Tommy was fourteen at the time, in the same class, and James had hated him all through elementary and high school. Tommy had always picked on James and thought himself quite the big shot, because his dad took him hunting and he played football for the school.

Tommy was a little overweight, double chinned, but thought he was good looking. Apart from being a bully, he also thought he could touch all the girls wherever, and whenever, he wanted. Then he went over to the farmhouse one day, when he knew that James wasn't around, and shot Johnny Deer. Leaving the body to rot after hacking off his young antlers.

James hadn't known it was Tommy until he bragged about it at school, telling everyone how he'd stalked the deer through the woods for hours on end, to get just one shot. That had been all he needed, as he was a hunter, and an expert with a rifle in his hands. Now, the antlers were mounted on his wall along with all his other hunting trophies.

The truth was, Johnny Deer was close to the farmhouse away from his grazing family, and the 'expert' shot had poured almost a dozen bullets into his body before he finally collapsed. Then he butchered away at the head of the body to retrieve the antlers, not concerned at all about leaving the carcass, as he'd ridden there on a bicycle. It hadn't even been hunting season, or in an authorized hunting area. Tommy may as well have shot someone's pet dog or cat, as that was how close James felt about him.

James was used to crying, but having to bury his dear friend made him wail and sob like at no other time or since.

Whenever he recalled it, James could still see the bullet riddled body, Johnny's poor ravaged head, and Johnny's grieving family trying to push his lifeless body back up.

Tommy had moved away from home after they both finished high school, and James found him years later in a double wide trailer in Fresno. Tommy was a bigger slob now. His beer belly cascaded over the belted, dirty shorts that could barely get over his hips. A sleeveless stained vest revealed his flabby arms, various tattoos, and hairy armpits. Short, greasy, brown hair hung limply over his forehead and unshaved skin. Outside his very scruffy home, was his truck, a Ford,

6

dirty and as well kept as its owner. Stickers on the back window stated his love of hunting, guns, and the Raiders.

James knew he worked sometimes as a mechanic, and that his two grubby kids and similar wife were out. The kids in school, and his wife at a nearby café cooking fries and burgers. The kids looked and acted like their father. Their foul mouths mimicked their parents, whose favorite word it seemed was fuck.

Tommy was a man of habit. Virtually every day, at the same time, he would drive practically across the street to a strip mall, park his truck at the side of the liquor store, and buy a twelve pack of beer. These he would consume one after the other, sitting outside his trailer on an old plastic chair.

Neither Tommy or his family were popular on the trailer park. They threw their trash everywhere, and were very unfriendly. It looked like a junk yard around their beat up trailer, with old car parts, beer cans, and hundreds of cigarette butts. In comparison, the other trailers looked neat and looked after.

The only change to Tommy's routine was when his wife was home, and he'd send her to the store, or he had some work to do and couldn't stick to his normal daily habit.

He didn't have any work today, and he'd also put gas in the truck just a few days prior. That had been a worry to James, as he didn't want to have to stop at a gas station, although the destination was not far away. James had resolved to take along some fuel in a spare can until he saw Tommy put some diesel into his grimy truck.

Watching the time, James took out his bicycle and a blanket from the trunk of his car, then made his way over to the side of the liquor store. It was a deserted area with just the service doors to the shops on the strip. He waited quite nonchalantly for Tommy to arrive and pull up in the usual place. James looked like a regular cyclist in his helmet and riding gear, just taking a breather in the rather warm weather.

Tommy didn't disappoint. Wearing his normal, dirty, light blue baseball cap and its obscured logo, he pulled up, and left the truck unlocked while he went into the store. He emerged two minutes later with his box of cans and opened the passenger door to put them on the seat. As he was straightening up to close the door, James stepped behind him, and hit him heavily on the back of the head with the small weighted cosh that he'd taken from the zip bag on his handlebars. Tommy's face fell forward on to the seat and James bundled the rest of him into the truck, thankful now for all his training, as Tommy was a heavy lump. James positioned him lying half on the bench seat, with the seatbelt holding him secure. He looked like he was sleeping.

Finding the keys in one of his pockets, James put the cans of beer in the bed of the truck, closed the door on Tommy, then casually put his bike and blanket alongside the beer. There was a locked toolbox attached to the bed, and James suspected that Tommy kept his rifle in it. He then opened the driver's door and got in, looking in the mirrors and out of the windows for any sign of witnesses. Not that it would matter, he was well disguised, but he didn't want a cop car to start following him, or worse, a curious witness.

James didn't drive long before stopping in a turn out with good cover. There he secured Tommy's wrists and ankles with plastic zip straps, and covered him with the blanket that he'd brought along. Tommy could well have seen the cyclist and may have even wondered why he had a blanket with him, but James doubted it, as Tommy never gave him a glance. James drove away again with Tommy still out cold, crumpled now into the space between the seat and the dashboard.

He knew the place he was taking Tommy was unstaffed at the moment, and would be for many more hours. It was also remote, private, with no security cameras, which was very important. It didn't even have a paved road to it, just a dusty dirt track, and all visitors were by appointment.

After he pulled up, he used one of his various skills and opened the lock on the main gate, driving the truck through, but leaving the lock looking secure after he closed the gate behind him.

He was able to drive within yards of his destination, where he manhandled Tommy out of the truck and cut off the ankle binds, leaving Tommy balanced with his back on the hood. He didn't bother taking off his disguise. Tommy wouldn't recognize him even if he did, and finding a water hose he turned on the faucet and sprayed Tommy's ugly face.

Tommy came to with much swearing, many threats, and he was scared.

"What the fuck do you want? Where the fuck am I? You're going to die you mother fucker. What's going on?"

"Hi Tommy," replied James pleasantly, "I want you to apologize. We're in a private wildlife park if you haven't noticed."

"Apologize? What the fuck for? Who the fuck are you?" bellowed the truly outraged Tommy, whose face was slowly going purple.

"Don't you recognize my voice Tommy? I'm James Wrigley."

"Who? I've never fuckin heard of you. What do you want? Where are we?"

"Oh come on Tommy boy, we went to school together, we were in the same class. Don't you remember beating me up virtually every week, tripping me up, calling me names, dunking me in the toilet, throwing things at me? Oh yes, not to mention killing my deer and taking its antlers that you hung up on your wall. You don't remember me Tommy?" He mocked.

Tommy looked at him more closely, struggling with his hands behind his back.

"The pathetic kid from school? You look nothing like him. Now let me go before I kick your sorry ass again."

"Times change Tommy. I am rich and successful now and you're what? Oh yes, you're a bum and your family is as sorry as you are. You still hunt defenseless animals?"

"I hunt and I'm going to kill you. Is this what this is all about?" Tommy was slowly remembering. "Your fuckin stupid deer?" I hunted that deer and I shot it. I did nothing wrong, it was a wild animal. Now let me go!"

"Hunted? My deer would have walked right up to you and you pretend that you hunted him. If he'd been truly wild your fat ass would never have got near him, and your rancid odor he'd have smelt a mile away. He was my pet Tommy and you damn well knew it. Then you go bragging about it and continued to persecute me throughout the rest of my school years. Now I want you to say sorry for everything you did to me."

"What? Apologize to you? Go fuck yourself, and let me go before I do something really bad to you."

"You know something Tommy? I had a feeling that would be your response. I just wanted you to show some remorse and to give you a chance"

"I'm not sorry for anything." Was the defiant reply.

James walked up to him and avoiding his legs, he punched him hard on the nose, breaking it, and Tommy screamed as his nostrils spurted blood.

"You are so going to die mother fucker!" Tommy yelled as the blood poured down over his chin, neck and chest.

James turned him around and forced him to walk to the nearby barred fence where he threw him down on the ground, before he opened the padlocked door. He left it open as he lifted Tommy and pushed him through, making Tommy fall again before closing the door and locking it. Tommy struggled to his feet and turned back to James, still cursing and threatening.

"So what's this you sniveling bastard. You lock me in a cage? Oh how scary you little pussy."

"Turn around Tommy and I'll cut off your wrist straps. This isn't a cage, by the way, it's an enclosure"

Tommy turned around and let him cut the plastic. "Who gives a fuck whether its a cage or a stupid enclosure. So you're getting frightened now are you and you're going to let me go? You are so going to die you mother fucker" and he turned threateningly to James who had stepped back from the bars.

"Actually Tommy, I wanted to see how good of a hunter you really are, but on an equal footing. You have company in there, hungry company that hasn't eaten for a couple of days. You may have noticed if you've looked around, that there are other cages and enclosures, with some wild turkeys, a black bear, coyotes, and some rescued circus animals. The one you're in is a little different, as the occupants have just arrived and they won't just take your teeth for a trophy. They will eat you piece by piece and I am going to watch. I think you'd better turn around Tommy, someone is wondering who you are."

Tommy turned around and almost fainted at the sight of the mountain lion that was coming towards him.

"Get my fuckin gun out of the truck!" Tommy screamed.

"The lion doesn't have a gun Tommy, so let me see you hunt him fairly. You can always pick up a rock and hit him with that. Because he has sharp claws and teeth, you can have my knife. It's a real hunting knife. Unlike the animals you normally kill Tommy, from a safe distance after you've been feeding them like a pet for months on end, this lion isn't a pet. He and his partner had to hunt for their food to live, and they were captured after almost getting killed by a hunter. So I'm giving them an equal chance with you Tommy, no guns for either of you. A fair fight. Are you ready to say sorry now?" He threw the knife down next to Tommy.

"Yes, I'm sorry, now get me the fuck out of here you son of a bitch!" Tommy was panicking but picked up the knife.

"Thank you for your apology Tommy, I really wanted to hear you say that. If you'd only said that when I gave you the opportunity earlier, then you wouldn't now be in the enclosure. I would have let you go. I really would. Now it's just too late. These are the consequences of your actions when we were younger, and your total lack of consideration for anyone but yourself. However, if you can defeat the lions, or they are disgusted with your taste and would rather starve, then I will let you go."

"Let me out of here you bastard. I have a wife and two boys, you can't do this to me"

"They'll be better off without you Tommy, you make everyone miserable. You're not exactly a role model are you. Your kids are just like you, loud and obnoxious bullies. You'd better watch out Tommy, the lion is getting closer. Oh and look, here comes his partner as well!"

Tommy turned around to see the male lion leaping at him and he went down quickly with the lion swatting at him, quickly followed by the female, cutting him to ribbons. Tommy screamed as James watched, feeling no sympathy whatsoever toward one of his main tormenters, as the lions easily dealt with him.

"This one is for you Johnny," James looked up at the heavens, "I hope you can rest at peace now pal."

CHAPTER 2

Edwin St. Clair still ran his IT Company with an iron fist, and his employees were always on alert for his arrival and subsequent mood. His business was very successful, and he'd made more than enough money to retire on, but even though he was almost seventy years old, he persisted in going in almost every day to oversee, and to make sure everyone was earning their money. He also liked to ogle all the young blondes that he preferred to hire, much to the annoyance of the male engineers, who were forced to do most of the work as their boss flirted with the females.

To his credit, he looked way younger than his years. Edwin kept himself in shape with a daily workout routine, and was always immaculate in his appearance. He spoiled his look by keeping the few remaining strands of hair on his head combed over, in a futile attempt of covering his baldness. He even dyed it, which just made it all the worse.

Apart from his hair, he was tall and trim, square jawed, bespectacled, but usually grim in his features. He rarely smiled or found anything remotely funny, unless it was a dirty joke.

Several months previously, he had married for the fourth time to a very much younger woman. Blonde, slim, big breasted, she had previously worked for him and he'd won her over with his wealth and promises. She now wanted him to get rid of his other blonde workers, as she was well aware that he would flirt, and one of the younger women would ultimately see her future in him. Just as she had.

Not that he listened to her. Edwin liked having a good looking younger woman on his arm and in his bed. As long as she kept compliant and her legs open, then he would indulge her a little, but not too much, as he was set in his routine and habits.

James knew Edwin St. Clair as he had once worked for him during his reformation. Edwin had always put him down him in front of

12

everyone, had given him the worst schedules, and had ridiculed and criticized his work even though James was by far his best engineer.

Despite being treated very poorly by Edwin, he learned a great deal about the IT business, computers, and the clients. That had been his sole intention upon taking the job, as he was adding to his skills. When he eventually left, he also had an undetectable route back into the system that he could access from anywhere, and he could also access all the clients' information. They would never know what hit them. The engineers would be far too busy looking for a new virus rather than an intruder that was already sleeping within their system. Edwin never scheduled anyone to specifically look for insider moles, he believed he was totally safe from computer viruses and hackers with the expensive protection he purchased.

James had hated working for him, especially when he yelled and cursed at him for not fixing a problem quickly enough. Edwin had an awful temper, it made the whole room shake when he got on a roll. James also hated that he was felt sorry for by the rest of the staff, who were thankful it was him, rather than them that was continually persecuted and belittled.

Edwin's new wife, Trudy, no longer worked, which was fine with her as she never liked it anyway. Having some of Edwin's riches at her disposal made her wifely duties more palatable.

She knew though that she needed to keep in shape, otherwise she would be out the door. As he'd made her sign a premarital agreement, she didn't want to be broke again, or jobless, so she went swimming virtually every day.

She could have swum at home, but it was lonely there. Instead, she had enrolled at the YMCA. They had a 50 meter pool so she could do her laps, but also have company during her keep fit routines in the gym. She also wasn't averse to being looked at by younger men.

James knew her routine as he had also become a member of the YMCA, three years after leaving the company. James had stayed in the area, not always in the same place, playing the stock market with no lack of success, after what he'd learned from being able to legally access company computers. Trudy had joined Edwin's company after James had left, as a receptionist, and James had seen a picture from their wedding in a newspaper. It gave him an idea.

James swam in a distant lane to her, but he also did laps. They had exchanged smiles and greetings for several weeks but nothing more, although he had noticed that she'd started to wear waterproof cosmetics, and her costumes get less practical.

He thought she was in great shape for her age, although in truth she wasn't that much older than James was. He suspected some surgical help, but her cheekbones were still sharp, no double chin, or that many facial lines. Her blonde hair wasn't long, barely shoulder length, and she brushed it back from her face. She did have flared nostrils, which made him wonder if she'd sniffed too many drugs, but she didn't appear to be an addict, as her fair skin was unblemished apart from a small tattoo on her right ankle of a red rose.

The biggest thing that surprised him, apart from her sleeping with Edwin, was her laugh. He'd heard it the first time when she was chatting to another woman, and he couldn't help but turn around when she emitted her deep, guttural laugh, that was the last thing you suspected could come from such a slight, yet very fit woman.

James had finished his laps and he was stood in the shallow end of the pool leaning back against the wall with his arms outstretched, watching the activity. It was a very quiet day for the YMCA. Some days it was hard not to swim into people, but this day, there were just half a dozen mothers teaching their babies, and some elderly swimmers slowly going about their routines.

He'd been admiring her pert rear as she effortlessly swam from end to end, and when she stopped four lanes away from him, he smiled and gave her a wave, which she returned. James didn't move. These days, he was confident and assured in his worked, and paid for body, and mentally, he had almost no fear left. It even surprised him sometimes when he was reflective. He could see she was obviously mulling something over as she cooled down, but then she seemed to find her answer and backstroked over to him.

James knew this was intentional, she could have easily just waded, but she wanted to showcase her breasts and James was happy to admire them.

She got to her feet directly in front of him. She was shorter than he but not by great deal, and her smile was genuine as she held out her hand and introduced herself.

"I keep seeing you here so I thought it was time to say hello properly. My name is Trudy St. Clair and it's very nice to meet you."

Her voice was a little low which may have explained the dirty laugh she possessed, but she had vivid blue eyes and looked sensational in her yellow one piece costume. The tepid water had made her nipples hard, and they pushed out the fabric of her swimming suit to great effect.

"It's a pleasure to meet you too. I have to admit that I've been admiring you from afar, but my name is Will, Will Young."

He shook her outstretched hand which was long and quite strong, feeling her sharp nails touch his wrist.

"You've been admiring me?" she asked, her hand still in his.

"Oh yes Trudy, for many weeks now, you are a wonderful swimmer." James smiled.

She giggled and took her hand away, a little reluctantly he thought.

"I thought there for a second you were making a pass at me."

"You're a very beautiful and sexy woman Trudy, and a I really enjoy looking at you. Your husband is a very lucky man and I hope he knows it."

Trudy self consciously felt her wedding band as he said this, turning it around her finger.

"Oh, I don't know. He should be as we haven't been married that long. Are you always this forward Will? "She replied with an amused expression.

"No. I just resolved to myself some time ago, that if ever the opportunity arose to express myself, honestly, with someone I found very desirable, then I would tell them. However, I would never have been so forward to swim over to you and said, 'excuse me madam, but would you care to come home with me this afternoon?' That would never have happened, especially as you wear a wedding ring. But as you came over to me, the least I can do is let you know that I find you very beautiful, and extremely sexy" James spoke softly, but let his eyes wander down to her still aroused nipples.

Trudy didn't move or try to slap him. He thought she blushed a little. She didn't stop him looking her over.

"I'm a married woman Will, and older than you."

She was standing her ground but she also wasn't saying no.

"I know that Trudy, and your age doesn't matter to me. I'm just letting you know what I think, and if you are offended, then I'm truly sorry, but it's the truth. I think we all like compliments whether we're married or not. I know I do. You can either shake my hand and walk away, then when I see you next I will just wave to you and bear you no ill feelings whatsoever. Or, you can kiss me, here and now, and we spend the afternoon together, just having some fun. I really want to kiss you Trudy, but if you don't want me to, that's your prerogative."

He watched her as she made her mind up, the water dripping down her face from her hair, looking around the pool at the other swimmers.

Finally, she took a deep breath and ducked under the water. James felt her hands go to his hips pulling him down, and he met her warm lips underwater.

James's home at that time was a rented furnished apartment, that he explained away by saying he was still waiting for all his furniture and belongings to be shipped from the East Coast. Trudy didn't question it. After the first frantic coupling, Trudy liked the attention she got and being made love to again, passionately, after having her husband give it her in the ass most times. She told Will about him, how boring it was in his company, the mistake she'd made in marrying him, but now she felt stuck. James was also able to glean other information from her purse that he needed. He enjoyed screwing St. Clair's wife. She was quite the temptress and agile in his company.

As James played with Trudy during the days when she was supposed to be swimming, he worked on her husband's finances at night, and on his other ongoing projects.

When James left St. Clair's employ, he'd asked Edwin to apologize to him for all the mistreatment he'd been subjected to. He hadn't been at all surprised when he received another mouthful of abuse and put downs. He wasn't going to ask Edwin to apologize again.

It didn't take long before Trudy was telling James that Edwin was always in a foul temper at the rare times he was home from the office, but at least now he was leaving her body alone. James felt a little sorry for Trudy, he had nothing against her, and her husband wasn't telling her what was happening to him.

James's carefully concealed computer virus that he had made active, was shutting down all the systems, extorting money from the clients, and putting the funds in a partially hidden account of Edwin's. James meanwhile, was luring the clients to a company he had set up, and it was solving all of their problems. He was also letting them know that some of their money had been diverted to an account of St. Clair's. Even if Edwin threw out his whole network and replaced everything, James knew he would never delete his private file of very intimate photos and videos. It was his most personal file, off limits to everyone, and the virus secretly lurked there.

Within three weeks of first bedding Trudy, James had almost destroyed her husband's business. He'd wiped out his bank accounts, his portfolio had completely disappeared, and Edwin's secret account where James had put the embezzled money had been frozen. Every asset that Edwin had that he thought was safe, was gone, and when he finally told Trudy they had nothing left, that her credit cards were useless, she turned up at James's apartment in tears.

He had her return home to get her belongings and most especially her jewels. Although Edwin kept a tight rein on Trudy's spending, he did like to buy her expensive jewelry. When she returned with as much of her stuff as she could put into her car, he gave her an address to go to in San Diego, car keys, and a fistful of cash.

James told her that he would look after her, that credit cards would arrive by mail in San Diego in her maiden name, and that he would join her there after he had been away on business to Europe for a few short weeks. He also gave her a new iPhone, and told her that if she kept in touch with her husband he could well immerse her in his mess.

James helped her transfer the stuff from her car to the one he'd given her, then had her drive Edwin's car around the corner, and to leave the keys in it.

Neither James or Trudy thought their relationship was going to be forever, it had all been purely sexual, but they'd thoroughly enjoyed each other, so much so that Trudy wanted some loving before she left.

It wasn't true that Trudy would be in trouble, but she totally believed James. When the local television news cameras showed Edwin being arrested, as she and James lay naked and panting in bed, she was soon dressed and driving to San Diego.

She was oblivious to the fact that James wasn't spending one dime of his own money on her. He didn't want to ruin her and he'd savored the sex they'd had, just as now he was reveling in Edwin's public demise and total humiliation.

As James continued to watch further news coverage on his old employer, he couldn't help but say aloud, "All you had to do was say sorry, you butt fucker!"

CHAPTER 3

James was born in Redwood City, California and was named after his deceased grandfather on his mother's side. Wrigley was his father's last name, but he changed it to Scott when he was an adult. Scott was his mother's maiden name.

The one thing that James had been able to do, from a very young age, was to amuse himself. With his mother having to work many hours to make ends meet, he learned that he could deal with being alone and got to enjoy it.

He knew how much his mom loved him, and he adored her, but she wasn't able to spend as much time as she'd have liked with him because of her situation. His mom was a homely woman, she knew it, but all she'd ever wanted was a family of her own to raise. James's dad was no looker either, so when she married him she thought it was going to be forever. When her husband turned around one day and said he was going, it was devastating to her. She'd tried to have more children with him, at least one to make their family complete, and he'd always been a willing partner. If little James hadn't been around, she would probably have gassed herself, but then she resolved to devote her life to him.

The animals helped of course with James's loneliness, and best of all they didn't judge him on his appearance, so they were his friends.

Despite his mom's financial woes, she would always help a stray animal and they seemed to know that. Some would move on, but others would stick around, or she would see a sign about a lost pet and contact the owners. Of course, it was mainly cats and dogs, but sometimes a raccoon would appear, the deer, and an odd fox or two.

They just seemed to know that this was a safe haven, they'd be fed and watered, and that no harm would come to them.

So James would play hide and seek with them, cowboys and pirates, his imagination to the fore as the animals would either join in, or just watch with much interest.

After the deer was killed, he tried not to get too close to the animals, but it was difficult, as they were his main company and his only friends.

So James grew up with his animal pals, and a computer that was a big friend but always a mystery to his mom. He still though, had to go to school.

His biggest fascination, which would serve him well, was opening things. Even before he went to work for the locksmith he could practically open anything, and on the computer he was the same. He always wanted to get on the inside, but having read that could be dangerous, he was very careful. That was the cool thing with computers and the internet. They told you how to do it, and how not to get caught.

His mom brought men home sometimes, but he rarely saw the same one twice. He knew she was lonely most of the time without his dad, so he didn't mind. James was quite self sufficient. He could cook and feed himself, do the laundry, and fix things. He was generally in bed when him mom came home, who nevertheless would always go in to his bedroom and give him a kiss goodnight. If there was a man with her, James might bump into him in the morning, but that was about it. No one ever got serious with her.

It was a different story at school. Kids would tell him his mom was a ho, and even worse things, and he would save his tears for when he got home.

All through school, James kept to himself and tried to avoid everyone. His grades were always good or better, so the teachers didn't hassle him, but they rarely protected him, just ignored him.

The only other kid that James felt any affinity with, was a girl named Alice. They weren't friends, they usually sat on opposite sides of the classroom, probably because she too was perpetually bullied.

Although she also was frail and plagued with acne, her biggest fault to the other kids was her hair. Frizzy, big, red hair. If they didn't pick on James, then they would go after Alice, and although James and Alice never spoke to each other, the relief was evident on their faces when they were getting some respite.

James would sometimes see her being tripped up, or her books being thrown, or gum put in her hair. Just like himself, she would dash from room to room and hurry to her home after school.

James didn't have much time for his dad. He was aware that his mom with her warm heart and kindness wasn't that tough with him, at least as far as financial maintenance was concerned. That was his mom, that's who she was, so kindhearted, but to James's mind that did not excuse his dad. He should have helped more. Instead, he got his eye turned by another woman and wanted to disregard his existing family. He would have to come by sometimes, he'd tell James to grow up, and that would be about it. He never offered to send his son to college. He wouldn't pay his back payments, or deal with the bank. His new family were all he could deal with, and he just wanted to forget that his former wife and son were still around.

Until James's mom was killed by a drunk driver after she'd had to go to work by bus, and was walking home from the bus stop, James remained awkward looking. Although he'd grown, he'd never filled out, had his eyes fixed, or cleared up his skin. He was just a lanky, thin, sick looking young man.

Although he was angry at losing his mom so needlessly, and still hadn't gotten over it, he then wanted to change his appearance. So began his transformation. He moved a short way to the IT firm after finishing his online college degree, started going to the gym and the pool, had laser surgery on his eyes, got his skin cleared up, grew his hair a little, and gradually gained confidence. He also took karate lessons and learned how to invest. He looked in the mirror one day and hardly recognized himself, and with the investments he'd made he was rich. It was a very satisfying moment for him.

He wasn't a traffic stopper, but he was very fortunate in that he only inherited his parents best features. His father's blue eyes helped a great deal, and with his mother's nose and mouth, he had grown into a reasonably handsome man with a great physique, although James himself still saw the awkward young kid in the mirror sometimes.

CHAPTER 4

Catherine Lewis, or Catherine Jenkins as she was now called, still lived in Redwood City and not that far from James's former place of work at the Locksmith's. That was where James had first met her, when she came into the shop pleading for help, as she'd locked herself out of her car.

She could have called, but she thought that if she did it in person, they'd be quicker about it, so James drove her home and within seconds had opened her car. Although he had to charge her, she was so grateful that she asked James to have dinner with her, which he did, and she became his first girlfriend.

Although they attended the same school, Woodside High, Catherine was younger than he and he'd never seen her before, but she had just started her senior year when they met, and like himself, she was an outcast.

Tall and thin with not much coordination, spotty skin, greasy black hair that came to her shoulders, Catherine wasn't even very intelligent, so school was a struggle for her. What she did have going for her though, was a lovely face beneath the spots, and she was quickly growing out of her gawkiness.

James watched it first hand. She began to fill out in the right places, her skin lotion was clearing her acne, and as she started to get looked at, she found better shampoos and cosmetics.

James barely changed during this time, but it was her metamorphosis that eventually got him into training and to change his whole appearance. It did take an action by her, along with his mother's death, to make him determined to change himself.

Working at the locksmith's had taught James many things, which he hungrily took in, and he became very good working intricately with his hands. He was always practicing how to open locks with different tools, as quickly as he could, and the more difficult the lock, the more he enjoyed it. He wasn't taught though about girlfriends.

James was still socially inept and Catherine was almost the same, they were even awkward with each other. They touched each other, explored, giggled, but they never got to having sex although they came close on several occasions. James liked being with her, and as she filled out he got even prouder when he took her somewhere, even the comments he heard like 'what is she doing with that loser' not bothering him.

He never really noticed her being distracted or anything, it was only later when he could reflect, that there had been subtle differences in her behavior that he may have been suspicious of if he hadn't been so besotted. As it was, he was totally naïve and unprepared.

One of James's habits was to frequent the International House of Pancakes on Veteran's Boulevard in Redwood City. To him, it felt out of the way, the servers were pleasant and friendly, and he liked the food, no matter what time of day it was.

He took Catherine there many times. The servers seemed happy for him to finally have some company, and he felt comfortable in the restaurant.

This particular day he had to work during his normal lunchtime, changing a home's locks after the husband had been asked to leave, so James quite happily went and did the job. After he finished, he went to IHOP for a burger and milk shake, and he was almost finished when Catherine came in. She didn't seem to see him, and he didn't get up to signal her, as she was with someone, another guy, and James felt sick.

He watched as they took a booth and snuggled up to each other, kissing and fondling each other. From where he was sitting, he could see the guy's hand going under her skirt, and Catherine was allowing him to.

The server went to their table and she was giving backward glances at James. She knew Catherine from James bringing her in, and she wished she could throw her out or just strangle her, but she was a customer, and so she had to serve her.

After she took the order she walked over to James and said, "I'm sorry James, I feel so bad, is there anything I can do for you?"

James replied no and thanked her, saying he'd like the check as his eyes remained on Catherine and the guy. A jock it looked like with his build, his buzz cut blonde hair, and his general demeanor. James could spot them a mile away and Catherine had always said she disliked them. Now here she was, in their special restaurant, making out with one of them.

James put his money on the check and he could feel the servers' eyes on him as he got up. He knew they felt sorry for him and he wanted to dig a hole and disappear.

He had to walk close by the booth that Catherine was sitting at to escape his hell, and he thought she would be apologetic if she saw him. When she finally set her eyes on him it was with no remorse or embarrassment, it was with defiance. Like she had planned this.

She whispered to the guy with her, who then looked at James with contempt as he walked by, and declared, "She's with me now sucker, a real man. You have any problem with that?"

James didn't reply. He was too upset, too damned angry, and with a last disgusted look at Catherine he left the restaurant, never to return.

The jock had since been arrested and jailed for drug offenses, but James had no beef with him. He didn't even remain long with Catherine, and it seemed to James, whenever he saw Catherine, that she was working her way through the entire football team. She always seemed to be with a different player. His anger was solely directed at her.

Catherine eventually married one of the wide receivers after they both had been declined college entrance with low grades, and he became a plumber with a local Redwood City company, as she went to work at a nail salon. They had two children, both girls, and lived in a duplex, nothing seemingly of excitement or of interest in their humdrum lives.

James purposely bumped into her one day as she pushed her cart and struggled to contain her girls as she roamed the aisles in Safeway. She didn't even recognize him when he said hello, and he had to remind her who he was.

"James? You look nothing like how you were!" she looked closely, quizzically.

"I got better, just as you did. So how are you Catherine?"

"I'm fine thanks. So are you married now, with kids?"

"No, not yet. I thought I'd found the right girl a few years ago but she found someone she thought was better. Although that guy went to jail, she found someone else, and now has two children by him."

The implication was very clear but Catherine didn't want to bite. Instead, she wanted to find out why James was now buff and fairly good looking.

"What happened to you James? I haven't seen you around for ages"

"I got wise Catherine. I finally reached my breaking point when I got dumped in public by a girl I really liked, and since then my life has transformed. It's just a shame she didn't believe in me, as she would now be sharing my life."

He was giving her ample opportunity to say, "sorry," but she couldn't, or wouldn't.

"Well, that's a pity. So you're doing well James?" She asked, totally ignorant that his comment was about her.

"Very well Catherine, thanks. I invested in a few dot com companies and I got lucky I suppose, so I'm not complaining."

"Good for you James, I'm happy for you." Although she looked far from it.

James really wanted her to just apologize, or explain her actions in the restaurant, but she was reluctant to do so, or just too dumb.

"So how are you doing Catherine?" He asked with resignation.

"Oh okay. I'm married now and we have the two girls. The girls have very much taken over our lives, but its all good thank you, we're doing fine."

"I'm glad you're happy Catherine. It's good that you're doing well. It's great seeing you again after all this time, and you look really good."

"Really? I feel overweight and unattractive."

"No, you look great. I'd never have guessed that you have two children."

"Thank you James, you are too kind. But look at you. All filled out, no glasses anymore, you look fit and very handsome." She flirted.

"I found a gym is all. So family life is going well for you?" He asked.

"Yeah, like I said, it's all good." Catherine replied, not at all convincingly as she tried keeping a rein on her children.

"Your husband is a fortunate man Catherine. You still have a great figure and you're still very attractive. He must be very thankful for you."

Catherine gave James a look that seemed to say, 'yeah, right, I wish.'

" I need to go now Catherine, but it has been really great bumping into you after all this time. I don't think I've seen you since you were still in school and we used to go to IHOP. I do have to run though, but I do wish you all the best for your future."

"I hope I'll see you again James, it's been good to see you as well. I hope you take care of yourself." She answered, forlornly.

She wasn't for apologizing, so James let it be.

"Take care of your family Catherine, I'll see you later."

James left Catherine gathering her two girls as he left the store. She was still good looking and a woman now, but looked overwhelmed and very tired. She was not the gawky girl he fell in love with anymore, but he still couldn't understand her reluctance to apologize for the hurt that she knew she caused him. She could never have forgotten the humiliation she caused him in IHOP. She would be sorry.

A few years previously he had hired a high end escort and she had not only been very beautiful, but also extremely sexy and very accommodating, for a hefty price. She taught him how to make love and how to treat a woman. He'd kept in touch with her, still spent an odd night with her, and now she would prove her worth.

James rented a furnished apartment that she pretended to live in for a day, and she called the plumbing company that Catherine's husband worked for, asking for him personally to fix a drainage problem. The escort was long legged, blonde, very seductive, and had no problem whatsoever in enticing the plumber to have sex with her.

When he arrived, she opened the door in a short, flowery blue dress, low cut that showed her cleavage. It was difficult for him to avert his eyes from her breasts as she opened the door to him. She led the way to the kitchen, and he watched her ass sway, and her slim long legs stride like a model in her heels. Saying there was something blocking the sink, she watched as he tried to plunge it free before opening the cabinet beneath the sink. He could smell her scent and hear her breathe as she stood alongside him. Asking her for a bucket, she went to get one as he got his wrench out of his bag.

On her return, he felt dry mouthed as she handed the bucket over, and he put it under the pipe before undoing the u-bend. Nothing much came out, so he turned over on to his back to see what was in the pipe, moving the bucket out of the way. Finding a piece of material, he pulled on it, and it released the water sitting in the sink, getting him soaked before he hastily moved the bucket back.

He looked back to tell the lady he'd got it cleared, and she was standing directly over him with her legs either side of him. He could see her white and very brief panties.

"You got covered in dish water," she said, her voice like honey dripping off a hot spoon, "you should take a shower."

She didn't move her legs, and she was looking directly at him with her sparkling blue eyes, licking her light blue lips with the tip of her tongue.

"It's okay, I'm used to it" he replied, not wanting to move away from the view he was getting.

"Come on," she said moving away, "follow me."

He did so, watching as she turned on the shower and obeying when told to remove his clothes. When he stepped into the shower, he wondered if this was a wind up, and maybe all his friends would be waiting for him after he finished showering, to heap ridicule on him.

As he was toweling himself dry she appeared again, and handing him a condom said, "Let me say thank you."

Before he could say or do anything, she was signaling with a long finger for him to follow, removing her dress as she did so, totally naked now as she climbed onto the bed.

"What is your first name?" He asked, putting on the condom and still not believing his luck.

"You want to chat or do you want to fuck?" She asked.

He didn't reply, he was climbing onto the bed.

The plumber had thought that horny housewives seducing workmen was a myth, it had never happened to him or any of his colleagues. If it had happened with some ordinary housewife then fine, but this woman was gorgeous. He probably wouldn't have objected even if he'd known he was being filmed, maybe even have encouraged it to prove it to his friends and ask for a copy.

Not only was he being filmed, but he was also being audio recorded. So his comments about being ignored and undervalued by his now sexless, nagging wife, how good it was to be with a beautiful woman again who liked a man inside her, making him feel like a horny teenager again, was just heaven sent to James. Catherine's husband even told the beautiful woman to forget about the service charge, as this was the best job he'd ever had, or was likely to ever get.

James edited the movie to avoid using his friend's face, but she'd maneuvered the guy expertly into the most explicit positions, with many close ups of his very happy face.

Not only did he send Catherine her very own anonymous DVD, he also posted it on YouTube for the whole world to see. Compounding her misery, her embarrassment, and utter humiliation. It was the least he could do.

CHAPTER 5

Michael Dowd thought he had it made. He'd worked his way up the banking ladder and was now being rewarded with millions of dollars in bonuses. He had an office on the top floor in the city, which enabled him a fantastic view of San Francisco. His family was set for life. He was able to play all the top golf courses in the world, hang out with celebrities at pro-ams, and screw some amazing young women along the way. It was great being rich.

Like many newly rich people, he thought he had done it the hard way with a tough upbringing, so fully deserved everything he'd gained. His idea of a tough life was being denied a sports car on passing his driving test, and having to drive a boring new suburban: not being able to choose his own vacations and having to go with his family: not getting his own credit card until he was twelve, and having to do his own homework (although he regularly paid someone to do it for him)

That his parents were able to pay for his complete education, give him a generous allowance on top of that, not to mention the homes, cars, clothing and credit cards, he totally disregarded that as just being normal. He knew many people who had it way better than he did. Compared to his fellow students while still at school, his family was positively poor, which was very embarrassing.

He now though had a home in Atherton, an apartment in the city, a house in Aspen, memberships in very prestigious golf clubs. He could use one of the company jets, and now he had his coveted sports car, along with several other vehicles. Life was good and he looked forward to every morning, as it just kept getting better.

Thanks mainly to his father's connections and school colleagues, he was able to rise quickly up the banking ladder, and he learned early that the top management liked ruthlessness and the profit line. Michael had no problem with that. He never believed peoples personal problems. It was all black and white, and it was every American's duty to pay their debts no matter what the price. He'd never had a problem, so why should anyone else? He really thought that he'd had it as tough as anyone, so no-one could pull the rug over his eyes. It was all bullshit.

Like many rich proud Americans, Michael preferred to avoid taxes so he was always moving his money around, mainly to offshore accounts. He had to be careful about it as he knew he could get into a ton of trouble if he got foolish. He also got philanthropic, which delighted his wife as it made them look good in the community and gained them awards, but it was really to avoid paying taxes. Although he was a staunch Republican, he hated paying anything to any government, so to give his tax money to charity and garner recognition amongst his peers was much more up his alley. The government don't hand out awards to big tax payers, but charities do to donators, and they make a big fuss of it with pictures and stories in the papers and magazines.

Michael wasn't at all good looking but he didn't know that. Overweight, not very tall, ruddy cheeked, a large nose, and small brown eyes. His brown hair was parted down the left side, and always looked greased down. He was able to dress well, his suits were fitted, shirts hand made, so he looked as wealthy as he was. His riches had got him a gorgeous blonde wife, and two twin girls who were equally as attractive as their mom. Privately, he thought his wife was as dumb as shit, although he'd never married her for her brains. She still looked great on his arm and in his bed, and that was all he really cared about. For her part, she didn't care how he earned his money, just as long as he had it and she could spend it.

Years previously, he had been put in charge of the loans at the bank that James's mom used. She'd taken over the mortgage from her husband when he left, but his reluctance and failure to keep paying his due created severe hardship for her and James. She tried to keep up and mostly did, especially after James found a job and contributed, but when she got sick everything changed.

Despite her working as many hours as she could, she wasn't entitled to any health coverage, so doctor visits were kept to an absolute minimum. Then after suffering what she thought was a heart attack, she had to have emergency treatment to remove her spleen. It cost her almost six month's mortgage payments and the bank wasn't at all happy. James poured all he had in to help, but with the hospital costs and the time off she'd had to take, it still left a huge debt.

Despite all of her pleadings and explanations, along with James's salary to help pay off the debt, the bank, or rather Michael Dowd, called her loan in and foreclosed their house. Michael Dowd was tough and unsympathetic, he didn't care that James's mom had been sick, so James and his mother had to move to a really bad part of Redwood City. Purely because Michael Dowd wouldn't alter their payments or defer them. There were many others that Michael Dowd had also foreclosed on, he had no time for hardship stories.

James hated banks and people like Michael Dowd. He hated him so much that even an apology wouldn't be enough from him. All Michael Dowd cared about was profit, his own well being, with no thought whatsoever to the hurt he and his bank did to people.

James had been working on him for quite some time and he'd needed all of his training and more to unearth all the banker's accounts. The domestic ones were fairly simple. He had a huge salary and an astronomical annual bonus that easily paid his mortgages, utilities, credit cards, domestic staff, luxuries and more. Money flew everywhere from he and his family, and it was but a drop in the ocean.

The real wealth was hidden in the offshore accounts. James guessed rightly that most of this money had come from insider trading. The payments were made from all over the world, some directly from the banker, but James knew that it would be almost impossible to prove, or to convict him for it.

He did though take control of it. When he found the electronic correspondence that the banker received on a regular basis about his holdings, James replicated them, then moved the money by a myriad of untraceable channels to his own account in Switzerland. He then ensured that the banker received updated mailings, so that he remained unaware of what James had done to him.

James wanted to do more. His memories of living in the poor part of town were almost as bad as school. It wasn't the bullies, it was the crime and the filth. Shootings almost on a daily basis, addicts pleading for money. Possessions being stolen, rats scavenging everywhere. The scary dark nights. His mom being killed there.

James didn't blame the other tenants. Everyone he got to know and spoke to wanted things to be better, but when you're in a hole it's very difficult to emerge. He even used his own skills sometimes, not just for the extra money it brought in, but mainly for protection. Being able to open things easily makes you many friends, who don't want you to get hurt.

Taking money from the banker wouldn't really hurt him that much and James really wanted to get him back. To put him in his own hole. The guy earned way too much money, he would recoup what he lost very easily off the backs of other unfortunates, and it needed to stop.

He'd seen the contract the banker had with the bank, and there was only one way. It would eliminate the bonuses, the salary, stock options and termination fee all in one go. He had to commit a felony.

James began a blog under the banker's name and hid its details on the banker's home computer, only blogging when he knew Michael Dowd was home.

It was very right wing, blaming everything on liberals and commies, and saying people should get to work and live the dream. Health insurance wasn't a right, it was socialist, and if you worked you got covered. Guns for everyone, no matter what type, and gays were abhorrent. The homeless were a blight and should be removed, permanently, by whatever force necessary.

James visited a gun fair shortly after starting the blog, and was able to obtain, without showing I.D. and paying cash, several illegal automatic weapons. It was so easy it was criminal, and they even provided hundreds of rounds to go with them. These he deposited in the banker's home one afternoon, when no one was home, hiding them well.

Michael Dowd's biggest love, apart from his own reflection, was golf. He adored the game, the private clubs, the connections, the famous people he got paired with and could brag about.

He played every weekend but also played on Wednesday's. He would go into work in the morning, then go and have lunch and play eighteen with his buddies before having a few drinks to finish off. It was only a short drive home from the neighborhood club through quiet streets, and there was never a problem. He enjoyed Wednesday's immensely.

James bought a prepaid phone just to be careful, and a few nights previously he befriended a very sick homeless guy with a shopping cart not very far from the banker's home. He told him that he would be able to give him a few things, mainly some cash, if he would meet him the following Wednesday night. The gaunt man was only too willing.

The street the banker lived on was like many in the Atherton neighborhood, it was dark and there were no sidewalks. Whoever designed it presumably thought the rich never walked or needed street lights.

The banker had really had a good day. The profits had gone up at the bank again and he'd played well in the golf game, winning most of the skins. A few shots of malt whisky afterwards and he felt elated. Hungry for dinner at home, and a jump afterwards on the compliant wife. Driving home, he never saw the homeless guy until he flashed into his vision and he plowed right over him.

He stopped many yards further, the sensation of running over someone making him feel sick, and the screech of something as he did so making it worse.

He climbed out of the car and walked back, seeing the tangled remains of a shopping cart and the mangled body of a dirty unkempt man. He didn't know what to do. He looked around and there was nothing to be seen or heard. The guy, he thought it was a guy, looked dead, no movement. Like a lumpy blanket dumped on the street. He looked around some more. Then he ran. He ran back to his still running car and drove away. He wanted no part of this mess.

James, after pushing the guy and his cart into the path of the speeding car, had quickly disappeared behind a nearby wall. He was able to watch the banker unseen as he stopped, then ultimately drive away, not even checking to see if the man was still alive. James did, checking the homeless man for a pulse on his wrist and neck. There wasn't one.

James then ran too, in the opposite direction, before stopping and calling 911 on the prepaid phone, panting as he gave the information. He told them he'd been cycling and saw this car mow down somebody, at speed, and then drive away. He'd followed the car on his bicycle to an address not far away. He gave the house address, the car make, license plate, and then said he had to go as he thought he'd been seen.

James took the phone apart, dumping it in a trash can by the nearby restaurant where he'd parked his car.

James felt really bad about the tramp, but he'd only picked him because his sign had said he had terminal cancer. He had even told

James that when he'd spoken to him, and that his life was pure agony, every day. He'd become homeless after he'd lost his job, and was then diagnosed with the cancer. It was eating away his intestines and without health insurance and no family to support him, his days were numbered. The pain was such, that all he wanted was to be put out of his misery, or to just get drunk enough to forget about it for a few hours.

On the following day's news, they reported from the crime scene that a very prominent local banker had been arrested.

James went to the local library, and in the comment section of the San Francisco Chronicle after their report, he asked if this was the same Michael Dowd who blogged about liberals and how un-American they were. He left Michael's blog address.

He then left it alone, noting the police searched his home, and although the banker was released on bail, it was plainly obvious that he was in serious trouble. James delighted in watching his downfall, seeing his money dwindle to nothing when the bank first suspended him, without pay, then ultimately fired him. He had watched in the courtroom when he was found guilty of manslaughter, leaving the scene of the crime, driving whilst intoxicated, and illegal possession of firearms. James wasn't worried about Michael's wife and girls. They were very attractive and would be okay. Michael's parents were still wealthy, as were his wife's. They would just hate their husband and father for the rest of their lives for embarrassing them, and killing someone whilst drunk.

Michael Dowd's downfall was very satisfying to James, and he anonymously donated more than enough money so that the homeless man had a good burial and headstone, along with a sizable sum to a local shelter.

CHAPTER 6

Alice Waters too had transformed, but unlike James, hers was purely natural. It had just taken time. Alice had been James's classmate during high school on the other side of the room.

She had gone to college after high school but it had been much the same, the same names, the same treatment, and the same isolation. That was just after the first year, which was so bad she wasn't even able to talk about it for many years.

She concentrated on her studies, but it wasn't until she was about to graduate with her medical degrees, that she felt she began to transform. It had started earlier, but not in her own eyes. She'd felt exactly the same. Then she started being approached by former male tormentors who now wanted to date her, and the female tormentors looked at her with envy.

By that time, she had no respect for any of them, they had largely ignored or abused her for years, so she just wanted to get away from them and start her career.

Her family still lived in the Bay Area and she had nothing but love for them. Her parents had struggled to send her to college, she knew they had little money, but they had insisted to realize her dream. She could only guess how much they had borrowed, but they never mentioned it, or ever showed regret for doing so. Alice's brother was now in high school, he was a red head as well, but Alice had no doubt that her parents would also send him to college as well. She didn't want to live too far away from them.

She applied and got an internship with the Stanford Hospital, which had a great reputation, and it was close to home. So with her grown up body and her straightened hair, she headed home, only now with a lot a backward glances from all the guys.

Alice had scars, not visible ones, just the ones that lurk under the surface. She found it hard to stay in relationships, her reflection not registering with her subconscious, so she was always looking at her younger self. Professionally she was very successful, but in her personal life, she wasn't happy at all.

She'd dated often at Stanford, and had spent nights with various partners which she'd enjoyed. She just didn't believe any of them when they said they wanted to see her again. She thought it was a wind up that was only enforced when she looked in the mirror and saw the same girl from college and high school. She was just being teased again, and eventually they would let her down, just like everyone else had. It was very rare when she saw anyone a second time, and if she did, it didn't go to a third.

Her parents knew she was having a problem and they kept telling her how beautiful she was, how proud they were of her. They had always told her that, so it never altered her thinking.

It wasn't as bad for her brother, as he was athletic and popular. He got teased for his hair, but as he was now an integral part of the football team, his was just friendly ribbing. Not that he could differentiate, he hated it. While his sister was in college, he'd been in middle school and had to defend himself from the assholes who wanted to beat him, so he learned to fight and give back as much as he got and more. If he came across anyone in high school who was being subjected to unfair behavior, and they were unable to defend themselves, he would step in and protect them. Alice was very proud of him, and wished there were more kids like him at other schools.

Alice threw herself into her work, pinning up her gorgeous red locks and hiding her figure under the white coat, still not ready for a life beyond school and her vocation.

She was a huge success at the hospital and was now the chief pediatrician. Her work and reputation was second to none, and after all the help her parents had given her, she was happy that she could now help them out from time to time.

Not that they wanted it. They were very proud, and it was only with reluctance when they accepted, but she knew that she owed them a lot.

Her parents thought it would be a good idea if she attended the upcoming high school reunion. The invitation had been sent to their house as they had never moved, and Alice kept her address secret from anyone in her past. Alice hadn't attended any reunions over the previous years, she had no friends there, so never saw the point. Her family thought it would help her to go, that seeing her tormentors not having improved would be cathartic.

Alice didn't think so but promised to think about it.

They told her to just go, walk around, then leave. Five minutes tops and she'd be on her way home. She wouldn't even need to speak to anyone.

Alice left it there, very much undecided.

CHAPTER 7

Martin Hughes was a builder and he used to be a total idiot. That was just his opinion. The people who knew him called him worse things, and if he knew what those things were, then he would have agreed.

Despite being married to a wonderful woman and having two terrific boys, he did his level best to screw it all up.

His downfall had been drink. Drugs as well, but mainly drink. What started out as just hanging out with the guys and drinking a few beers, developed into many joints of weed and gallons of booze. Every day. Then he would lose jobs for not showing up or arriving still drunk. He thought it was cool at the time and that the employers were just assholes. He was in control and he could handle it, he was just having fun.

He would make good money when he worked, but when he didn't, he would spend what he had on himself at the liquor store. His wife and two boys would be left to get fast food rather than fresh produce, as that was their only option. Martin had to have his booze and he didn't care if anyone suffered.

It began to wear on his wife. Bills wouldn't be paid and she and the boys would be left short. Martin meanwhile would be whooping it up with his buddies in the garage.

The rows started and she didn't want his stinking drunk body on top of her anymore. It was after one such altercation that he'd gotten into his battered truck and went for a drive.

His memory was still fuzzy, but he managed to drive to the other side of town and then he woke up handcuffed to his hospital bed.

He thought it was just the worst hangover ever, but he was hurting all over his body. He discovered later that his forehead had collided with his windscreen because he didn't wear his seat belt, but that he was extremely lucky that it had only caused forty five stitches and not cracked his skull. His ribs had smashed into the steering wheel and one of the six broken ones had perforated one of his lungs. One arm and one leg were broken, and the other leg had a broken ankle. He had cuts everywhere, and was informed that his liver was almost shot from the drink. He'd also dislocated his wrist on the broken arm. He ached everywhere.

After the doctor explained all the injuries, then came the worst part. He was told he had passed out at the wheel and had slammed into a waitress walking home. He was shown the photos. She was just yards from her home when his truck mounted the sidewalk at speed and crushed her into a concrete wall. He saw himself slumped over the buckled steering wheel and the cracked windscreen. It was an older truck and it didn't have airbags. The front wheels were flat from bursting after he hit the sidewalk. The hood was caved in and crumpled, with the top half of the woman lying on what remained of it.

The cops who told him this had waited for three days for him to wake up, so angry at him for driving drunk, and especially for what he did to that poor woman.

He'd almost separated her upper body from the rest of her and she'd bled out over the hood. The cops were almost in tears as they showed him the carnage he'd caused to the woman, that they had seen at first hand.

They told him that when they were finally able to pull the truck away from her, the lower half of her fell to the ground as her torso remained on the hood.

Martin couldn't remember any of it apart from driving away from home angry, heading to the other side of town. As they passed the gruesome photos in front of his eyes, one by one, he saw himself looking lifeless in the driver's seat and the woman dead on his hood. He couldn't deny the evidence.

When his wife arrived, all he could do was say sorry and that he would make it up to her. He had been a fool and that it was he who should be dead, not that innocent woman. Martin pleaded for her to give him another chance.

When he eventually made it into court after being in hospital custody, Martin was in a wheelchair and still looked like a train wreck. Ignoring his attorney's advice, he pleaded guilty to everything, but he felt the judge was way too lenient in only giving him eight years.

After the sentencing, the judge asked him if he wanted to say anything, and after earlier being told who her son was, he apologized for his stupid and reckless behavior.

Martin's wife and the two boys moved in with his parents, and he instructed them to hand over any proceeds, if there were going to be any, from the sale of their home to the deceased woman's son, with his profound apologies.

Martin only spent five years in jail. He was a model prisoner who took guidance and started to attend church.

On his release, his parents helped him restart his building business, and eventually he was able to move his family into a new home. His wife, amazingly, stuck by him, and he was determined not to screw up again. He stayed away from his old friends, alcohol, and the weed, but was still tormented by nightmares of the crime scene photos.

The woman he'd killed was called Ellen Wrigley, James's mom.

Martin was neither handsome nor ugly, just somewhere in between. He was 5' 10" with short brown hair that was rapidly receding from the forehead. He weighed around 240 pounds, and couldn't get rid of the belly he'd acquired before going to prison. His face was clean shaven, with brown eyes and a piggish nose, along with a nasty scar on his forehead. Whenever he went to the bathroom, the scar always reminded him of what he'd done. Martin now walked with a slight limp, and his wrist was prone to a little arthritis if the weather was cold.

Once a week, usually Friday, Martin liked to escape his diet and have a big breakfast at Denny's. He would dine alone and sit at the counter. James knew this when he sat just a seat away from him, and engaged him in conversation.

James wanted to know what was good on the menu, if the weather was going to change, how the 49ers would do, what he did for a living, and if business was good.

Eventually, Martin introduced himself and handed over his business card, but his face changed color when James told him his name was James Scott, but that his last name used to be Wrigley.

Martin stared at him. He remembered vividly the frail young man in court who was overcome from grief, but this man barely resembled him.

"Were you related to Edith Wrigley?" he asked, afraid.

"She was my mom."

Martin's face went whiter, now he was scared. He kept on looking at James who was signaling the waitress for some coffee and to order.

"I'll have the two eggs over easy, with bacon and sausage please, and an English muffin. I'll also have coffee with some cream." He told her pleasantly.

She poured his coffee and passed him a bowl full of individual half and half's before tapping his order into the computer screen.

Martin had just eaten his breakfast when James had sat down, otherwise he would have pushed it away.

"Are you going to kill me?" he asked. "Is this why you're here?"

"Are you drinking again?" James enquired.

"No. I haven't wanted to ever since I" he paused, "since your mother."

"That's good" replied James, a little coldly.

"I will never be able to express just how sorry I am for what I did. I go to sleep and most nights I see the photos in my mind of what I did. I'm not the same person now but it doesn't bring your mother back. For that, I'll be eternally sorry, but if you wish to kill me, I would understand. If our situations were reversed, I would probably want to kill you. What I did was truly awful, there is no excuse, I was a total jerk who let everyone down."

"All I ever want" said James, taking a sip of coffee, "is for people to apologize for what they did to me that was wrong. You did in court and I know you meant it. It has changed you. You did the very worst thing to me, Martin, but you showed remorse in court and that hasn't changed. As long as you don't go back to drinking and driving Martin, I forgive you. But if you do, then you'd better look over your shoulder. I won't allow you to kill someone else's mom."

Martin absorbed this, and took a couple of minutes before replying.

"Then you have my deepest gratitude Sir, and all I can add is that I am still deeply sorry for what I did. I won't go back to drinking. I like being sober and being a husband and father again. You know who I am, and you obviously know how to find me. If there is anything, absolutely anything that you ever need, call me. Anytime, any day. Thank you sir, from the bottom of my heart."

James looked over at him and Martin was almost crying, he was trembling.

"Take care of your family, Martin, and yourself." James held out his hand which Martin took and shook as he stood up, dropping a $20 bill on the counter with his other hand for his breakfast.

"Thank you Sir, thank you."

Martin left as James's breakfast arrived, which he thoroughly enjoyed.

CHAPTER 8

James was still really living out of a suitcase. He had never decided where he wanted to live after getting wealthy, so he moved around from one furnished apartment to another. At the moment he was in Foster City, which was very near to Redwood City.

Trudy St. James was currently living in another of his rentals, an extended stay, but he would soon have to move her on. James didn't want her to be a permanent fixture.

He thought he would fly down to San Diego sometime, for one last fling with her.

It was easy for him to live like he did, but he did miss seeing his mom's furniture and knick knacks around. He'd kept it all in a storage unit for years now and sometimes went by to sit and reflect.

He liked his current apartment. It was bright, clean and modern. There was wireless for his laptop, and he could keep his fitness up with the exercise room and two pools. Not to mention the great view he had of water and a wild bird sanctuary.

He generally spent most of his days on the computer, researching and hacking. His list was getting shorter now. He still wasn't going through it in any kind of order, just randomly, and dependent on what he'd found out.

He also kept up with the local news. He wasn't on anyone's mailing list, he only kept a post office box, so no one sent him anything, which he was very happy about. He did see though that there was a school reunion planned at the Sofitel Hotel in Redwood City. He thought he would go. Not to connect with anyone, just to see what they all looked like these days. There would also be a reason to be there. He called the number and added his name and year.

James drove a new Mercedes, and coincidentally, two of his antagonists now worked together in one of their dealerships in Thousand Oaks near Los Angeles.

The two had always been close, it was rare when you saw one without the other, but James didn't like either of them and never had done.

Like Tommy Hilditch, whenever they caught sight of James it seemed they did something to him that they thought was hilarious. Pushing him down flights of stairs, or slapping him around the back of the head, it was all the same to them. Even making James do their homework didn't let him off. They'd push his lunch into his lap, or take his glasses and throw them hard against a wall. It was never ending amusement to them.

When they graduated high school mainly thanks to James, he asked them to apologize for all they had done to him, and to thank him for doing much of their work. Their response was to grab James's own diploma and tear it in half between them, laughing hysterically as they did so.

Their names were Steve Taylor and Larnell Cooke. Steve Taylor had been the football quarterback and Larnell was one of his wide receivers. The quarterback was tall, blonde with a close cut, and blue eyes. He was also square jawed and popular with the cheerleaders. His best friend, the wide receiver, was also tall and good looking. Larnell was black and as insufferable as Steve was.

They both got football scholarships to UCLA because of their success at Woodside. Whether it was a case of too much partying or just not being good enough, neither got beyond the sidelines for the college.

Without having James around or some other luckless soul, neither of them graduated college and they went to work selling cars. Being cocky, confident and devious bode them well, and they believed they were the kings of the car lot.

Both of them were married now to very attractive women. They lived on adjacent streets. They each had two children, and they practically did everything together. From cheating on their wives, to going to sports games, to gambling. If one of them did something, then the other one was close behind.

James had been watching them from afar since they all left high school.

Like virtually everyone else, they had become overly reliant on their electronic devices over the years. They fell right into James's hands.

They spent money before they had it. They obviously kept their stay at home wives away from the finances, or maybe the wives didn't care. They went on weekends without their families, yet would pay for four dinners. A great deal of spending and a lot of juggling with credit cards. Best of all to James, they had a bookie.

From what James could determine, they had come out fairly even on their gambling, although there had been a few close calls. In one instance, they had been down 50 grand to the bookie, but then it just disappeared. He suspected they had handed over a top of the range car and altered the books.

James easily found the bookie. He was illegal, but his specialty was ensnaring the college players and getting their inside information. While they were in college he would hand over cash for their tips, take their bets, and as long as they didn't wager too much money, he would also let it ride if they lost. He made a ton of money from the tips. Once they left college it was a different story. If they bet, they paid, and he wasn't averse to applying a little muscle if the payments were late.

Steve and Larnell also liked to throw money around when they went to Vegas as well. It was probably a ploy to garner free rooms, and to also bed the most beautiful women, but sometimes they over stretched, and there was a lot more maneuvering with the credit cards.

Stupidly, but then they were arrogant, they placed bets with the bookie by text. James found that out by going to the showroom once to look at a car, and asking to borrow a phone as his was dead.

Steve Taylor had only been too willing to oblige. He didn't recognize James. After James returned his phone, he disappeared as soon as Steve's back was turned.

James now had 2 credit cards in their names with a good credit limit. They would never get traced back to him and he could easily place bets with the bookie. He just wasn't satisfied with getting them into a financial headache. He needed something more personal.

He knew from getting into the hotel's system they had booked two rooms next door to each other for the reunion. He toyed with the idea of filming them with one or more of the ex-cheerleaders that they would no doubt hit on. He also thought their wives must be fully aware of what they did on their various trips, they couldn't be that dumb. It was probably out of sight out of mind.

James booked a flight to Vegas with a return flight via San Diego.

CHAPTER 9

James had a blast in Vegas. Blowing someone else's money on the roulette tables was fun and very easy to do. He couldn't figure out why anyone ever bothered playing roulette unless they backed either red or black.

If ever of the two car salesmen wanted an investigation, then it would have to start with the surveillance from the casinos. James had managed to appropriate a decent disguise that somewhat resembled Steve Taylor, and he was confident that if someone looked at the video recordings then it would cause much inconvenience. It would be a huge hassle for the car salesmen until they proved they were elsewhere. He also found a seedy motel while wearing his disguise and paid for it with cash.

Once he'd maxed out their cards, he checked out of the motel, but stayed in a good hotel without his disguise for another night.

He then went to San Diego. Trudy was elated to see him and couldn't wait to show off her tan, new bikinis, dresses, tops and skimpy underwear.

James thought it prudent to let her know first, that the lease would end soon on the apartment. He then handed to her the new bank account details, telling her it was hers to do with as she pleased. As there was almost 2 million dollars in it, she was ecstatic. He didn't tell her that the money had come from her husband. He didn't think it was necessary, and Trudy didn't ask although she may have guessed.

James barely left the apartment for the next two days. Trudy had missed their sex, and she wanted to make up for lost time. She was removing his clothes while James was showing her the bank statement, and James happily responded. He still liked screwing his ex-bosses wife, and Trudy wanted to make her last moments with James unforgettable.

Flying back to San Francisco, he didn't think he would ever return to San Diego, although Trudy made it clear she would drop everything if he did so. He would just see what happened. There were far worse places to be than in Trudy's embrace.

Before he boarded the plane he placed some bets with the bookie, using a prepaid phone. He knew how they conversed with each other and he kept it in the same style. The bookie thought they knew something he didn't with their crazy bets, but he took them and spread them around. James threw the phone away.

For the short flight back to SFO James was on his laptop and thinking.

As his fingers flashed over the keyboard he thought again about planting cameras in the ball players' rooms. It would be easy enough but probably pointless. They would no doubt enjoy seeing themselves on camera humping former schoolmates.

He then thought about doing a "Carrie" on them. He could rig up a big bucket of slime, get them on the stage, and dump it on them. It sounded good to him but he didn't even know if there was going to be a stage, and even if there was, he would need so much time and access without being seen. Then he would need an excuse to get them up there. It wasn't feasible.

What he really wanted to do was beat them up. He knew it would be easy to do one on one, but against two they could strike a blow back. He liked the idea but he didn't want any tell tale signs on himself like a cut lip or something. To get both of them alone, one at a time, would be perfect, if he could pull it off.

He was still musing about this when he stumbled upon something in Steve Taylor's work computer. It took him by complete surprise and he gasped aloud when he saw it. He also looked around to make sure none of his neighboring passengers had seen it.

He quickly took a flash drive out of his pocket and saved it, and then sent the file to an email address that he could access, but would never be traced back to him.

As he closed up the laptop in preparation for the landing, he again realized just how stupid the two guys were, and why they had forced him to do their homework.

CHAPTER 10

Alice had said she was going to the reunion and had paid the fee, but she still wasn't sure, even as she got ready. She didn't even know what to wear.

Come on Alice, you're a professional, pull yourself together. This is stupid. It's just a school reunion dammit. You go through med school, all the exams, then an internship working god knows how many hours, and you're nervous about this! Jesus, you talk to rooms full of young doctors and you lecture in big halls. Pull yourself together and get through this. There is absolutely nothing to fear. Just stupid former schoolmates who've barely got a brain between them. Now get dressed and go!

She thought about wearing one of the dresses that she'd used to great effect when dating. Short and showing cleavage. The guys had taken great delight in removing it from her, in the dark, but she wasn't on a date and didn't want some asshole from school all over her. She got one of her suits out. The green one that matched her eyes. She teamed it with a pale yellow blouse and a gold choker necklace.

She'd already done her make up and washed her hair, and wondered for a long time whether to pin her hair up or let it go. She let it flow. She put some rings on her fingers and checked her nails. Being a doctor they were practical rather than decorative, but in good shape.

Alice thought that her suit might be too formal, but she wasn't planning on sticking around, as she was resolved to just taking a look and getting out of there.

She teamed her suit with matching shoes, more practical that enhancing, but they were comfortable.

Alice left her apartment with a huge deep breath, and drove herself to the hotel in her almost new Lexus.

Arriving at the hotel she pulled up at the main entrance and let the valet park her car, telling him she wasn't going to be staying long. He told her to have a good evening as he gave her a ticket, and jumped into the driver's seat and drove it away. She entered the foyer.

There were many people milling around, but Alice didn't really look at them as she followed the signs for the Woodside High School Reunion. It was in the ballroom, and as she approached there were long tables set up with individual names lined up in alphabetical order on the white tablecloths.

Alice hadn't known this, but there were three reunions, so the tables had the year of the graduation behind them, with several people helping everyone find their name and checking to make sure they'd paid.

Alice gave her name to the woman who assisted her. She had a name tag that read "Samantha Roberts." The name meant nothing to Alice, and presumably Alice's name meant the same to Samantha as she took off the backing and slapped the name onto Alice's chest.

Alice made her way into the huge ballroom and realized why they had three separate years, as the room was huge. A buffet had been set up on one side, there was a long bar on the other, and people were dancing and laughing on the large dance floor as the disc jockey played songs from the different years.

There were also tables around the floor, and people were eating and drinking at them. It was loud, colored lights were flashing, but there was just enough light to see the names and to recognize old friends. If you had any.

Alice made her way over to the crowded bar, and after waiting for five minutes was able to order a glass of merlot that cost her seven dollars. She left a dollar tip and moved away to the side, resolving to just have the one drink and then go, as that was her limit for driving.

As she stood against the wall drinking her wine, people would brazenly walk up and stare at her name, although some of the men took that to mean they could admire her breasts. None of the women spoke to her. They just looked at the name and went on their way, although Alice did recall some of them. She didn't want to exchange pleasantries. A couple of the guys who she'd also known, tried to chat her up, telling her how much she'd changed for the better. She shrugged them off.

Everybody it seemed was in clusters, and she kept hearing the expression "do you remember?" Alice felt nauseous. There only appeared to be one other person like herself who was totally alone, and he was leaning against the wall watching the dancers. Her drink was almost gone so she wandered down to him out of curiosity, although truth be told he wasn't bad looking to her.

"Oh my god" she exclaimed, "James Wrigley? Are you the same James Wrigley that sat on the opposite side of my class?"

James was waiting for the envelopes he'd scattered around to be opened. The words "To be opened" had been printed on them in large letters but he had yet to see anyone open one. A couple of women had come onto him that he'd known but never liked, so he waited.

The two football players had already been to the ballroom and as he'd predicted, they had quickly taken a couple of giggly women presumably back to their rooms. He had to wait for them to return.

James barely glanced at Alice and just mumbled "Hello."

"I'm about to go now but can I say one thing before I do?" she asked.

Taking his silence as a yes she went on, "I just want to thank you for taking some of the persecution away from me. I hate to say this, but when you were picked on I was left alone for a while, and you'll never realize how grateful I was for that."

She finally had his attention and he looked at her name.

"You know something?" he smiled. "I used to think the same thing about you. You saved me from a few beatings."

"If you hadn't been wearing a name tag, I would never have known it was you. I only came and said hello because you were alone like myself."

"It seems time never changes Alice. You look great by the way, and I would also have never have recognized you. I think this is the first time that we've ever spoken."

"You'd think that we had so much in common, we'd have been friends."

"I was running so much, just trying to stay out of everyone's way, that I never got to know anyone. Not that anyone wanted to know me." James replied.

"I know the feeling James. Listen, I have to go now but I'm glad I got to see you. You look really well. Didn't your wife want to come tonight?"

"I'm not married Alice. Still alone. What about you?" James caught a glimpse of the two football players returning with the blushing women, and heading towards a large crowd.

"No. Me either. I hope we bump into each other again James, but I really must go."

A ruckus had begun near to the large crowd and laughter was coming from there. Photos were being held up, practically all around the room now. The envelopes had been opened. Very quickly, the two football players had been circled, they were being laughed at, and they tried snatching the photos. One of the photos floated by Alice which she caught and looked at.

"You won't believe this James" she said looking at the photo. "Those two guys are gay."

"I heard they were married with children. Are you sure?" he asked.

"Well, maybe they like it both ways. Here, take a look for yourself." She handed over the photo.

What she didn't know was that James had cropped and printed the photos, and all the photos were different. There were also two women in some of the photos, and everyone had been photographed in various poses. All the photos were really explicit and the two jocks were mortified, especially of the ones in which they were screwing each other as the two women watched and took the photos. At the time they must have enjoyed it, their smiles lit up the frames.

"Didn't those two bully you?" Alice asked, as James smiled at the photo and their predicament.

"Yes, and this couldn't have happened to nicer guys" he replied sarcastically. "Let me walk you out Alice, I don't need to stay here any longer."

As they waited for the valet to bring their cars, James asked Alice if she would have coffee with him one day. Alice thought lunch would be better and she handed him her card, telling him to call sometime.

James's car arrived first, and she was surprised that he was driving a top of the range, brand new Mercedes. She'd looked at one herself so she knew what it cost. He waved to her as he tipped the valet and got into his car. She hoped he would call her.

CHAPTER 11

The embarrassment caused to the two football players was perfect for James. He was well aware that they would be able to dispute the credit card charges in Vegas, but the bets with the bookie would be a different matter. He had posted all the photos on their Facebook pages, so they would have to endure a great deal of ribbing and explaining. Not least from their wives and families.

At the party, James had also seen a couple of others from his list. They hadn't recognized him or spoken to him, and his efforts to bore holes through them with his eyes hadn't worked. One was called Teco Gervasini and the other was Jonathon White.

Teco, despite his name was pure American. Even as a freshman he was 5'9." Bulky and overweight with short black hair, he liked to throw his weight around, but only on smaller kids.

Jonathon White was another of the same ilk. He thought it was cool to ridicule the smaller kids, or provoke them in some way. Jonathon was a blonde haired thief mostly. He liked to take money off the small ones in front of his friends, and if they had none to give him, he would slap them around the head to make his pals laugh.

Teco was just nasty. He would walk up to James and just thump him in the face or drop something heavy on his foot. James knew he did it to other kids as well, purely for his own amusement. If he wasn't hitting, he was threatening, and he and Jonathon liked to call their victims queers, or puffs, or gay boys.

Teco had beaten James so badly once that his nose was broken, he had a split lip, two bruised eyes and a broken arm. One of the teachers had seen this occur, but the only thing he did was to send James home.

James's mom was furious when she got home and took James to the hospital. The following day she marched into the principal's office to ask who had done it as James wouldn't tell her. She demanded to know who the teacher was and whether the other boy had been expelled. Why also had James been sent home with an obvious broken arm? He hadn't even been looked at by the nurse. Who was going to pay for the hospital visit?

The principal was a wuss. He knew who all the troublemakers were in his school, but the parents were active members of the council, or the kids were on the football team or cheerleaders. To throw the kids out, he knew he would have to go against the parents or weaken the football team, so he did nothing.

He just told Mrs. Wrigley that they were children, it was an accident, it would never happen again, but he would reimburse her from the school funds for the medical costs. She was fit to burst, but she also knew that if she made a real stink about it, then James would be in an even bigger mess.

Jonathon was more sneaky. He liked to sucker punch and walk away, or push the kids behind James on the stairs so that they would fall on him.

Teco Gervasini was now a 6' 4" uniformed cop in San Mateo, and Jonathon White ran a franchised computer game store that sold and rented the latest trends in the industry.

They were both active on Facebook, and James had befriended both under an alias via the library. Teco and Jonathon weren't connected as they never were pals, so James had sent various questions to them and their friends.

Most of the questions were general things like how the Giants would do, or where to buy the best burger and so on. Then he would throw in something like "how do you deal with a bully?" or "my boy was beaten at school. You think I should get who did it?" James would just mix all the questions up then wait for the replies.

Most of the friends would respond by saying to just report it to the school, but some, like Teco and Jonathon, said they would deal with it themselves. They pointed out that they had never been bullied, nor their kids, and that it was always better to hit first, rather than wait to be hit.

James sent another question. "Would you apologize to a kid you bullied or did wrong to at school?"

It was a similar reply. Most of the friends said yes. The others, including Teco and Jonathon, said they had nothing to apologize for, and if they did hit anyone at school or were mean to them, then they deserved it.

James had his answer. Not the one he wanted, but now he could get it resolved.

CHAPTER 12

It was two days before Alice heard from James. She didn't think he would call after the first day.

James called her while she was at work and left a message, saying that he would like for her to join him for lunch at Nordstrom's. By the time Alice got to her message it was almost noon, and she was sure that James would feel like he'd been stood up. She called him in a fluster, and was relieved to hear that he was still waiting in the store, and had spent too much money already on clothing he didn't need.

Not having the time to do anything with her hair or make up, she took the quick drive to the store, and thought it hilarious when she saw James with all his shopping bags.

"I hope you realize this is the most expensive lunch I've ever had." He greeted her with a warm smile.

"Tell you what James. I'll cover the actual food."

"Okay Alice, you're on. I'm starving. You look wonderful by the way, and thanks for coming today."

"You're being way too kind James. I know I look a mess but thank you anyway. You look good yourself. You sure you needed more clothing?" She teased.

Alice still had her hair up, but she'd removed her white coat to reveal her long sleeved white top and black pants with walking shoes. The hospital was nearly always cold, and she also did a lot of walking. If she'd known she was going out to lunch, she would have dressed a lot differently.

James looked comfortable in a taupe golf shirt with off white slacks and matching sneakers, and Alice was relieved he wasn't in a suit and tie.

The weather was still warm this side of San Francisco and almost everyone around was dressed casually.

"I don't really like shopping, but while I was waiting for you to call I wandered around and found a few things I liked." James replied.

"Well, let's go and eat, and thank you for calling."

They made their way to the cafeteria and were able to obtain a table. If this had been the weekend the place would have been packed, but today was a good day.

Both had the chicken broth but James went with the steak sandwich, while Alice had the crab salad. The store also gave popovers with strawberry butter and they both devoured them.

"I was looking at the year book last night," spoke Alice between bites of food, "and it's just amazing how much you've changed. I would never have recognized you without your name tag."

"You blossomed too Alice," James replied after swallowing, "and it's great to have lunch with you."

Alice could tell that James had not only grown upwards, but he'd also worked out. There was no flab on him, his arms were thick and well defined, and she suspected that he was the same all over. Not like a bodybuilder, more like a track athlete.

"So tell me James, what have you been doing since you graduated. Did you go to college?"

James told her virtually everything. Losing his mom, his jobs, the online college, and his investments. Alice was fascinated.

"So if was to leave my laptop in my locked car, you'd not only be able to open the car, but you would also be able to get into my computer?"

"Yes, I would."

"So how would you get into my computer without the pass code?"

"Easy. I'd just hack into it."

"You can do that? Wow James, I've never met a hacker before."

They both laughed and then Alice looked serious.

"Isn't that dangerous and illegal?" she asked in a softer voice.

"It can be both. Sometimes people lock themselves out of their own computers by forgetting their pass codes. They make them very elaborate to foil identity theft, but then they need someone to hack in to recover their data when they forget the code. So then it becomes legal because you are being asked to do it. If you hack into companies or the government to steal or alter data, then they can trace you and arrest you for it. So that is dangerous. Unless of course you work for the government, and it's your job to do that, but it is kept secret."

"You learned all this in college and at the IT firm?"

"I started doing it at home while we were at school. I was always fascinated with how to get into things, and the computer told me how to do it."

"Were you as lonely as I was when you were younger James?"

"I never felt lonely at home. It was at school I was lonely. It was always a relief when the bell went and I could go home."

"I hated school" replied Alice. "If I hadn't been so determined to be a doctor then I wouldn't have gone to college."

"Was it worth it?" Asked James.

"Oh yes. I love my job."

"Isn't it hard to lose patients?"

"Extremely hard. At first I used to go home in tears whenever somebody died, especially as they are so young. You never get used to it, you just resolve to make their last days as pleasant and as pain free as possible."

"I don't know how you do it Alice, I really don't. I was a wreck when mom died, I couldn't imagine going through that every day."

"It's not as bad as it sounds James. So how was your lunch?" She asked, grinning.

James had just finished and was wiping crumbs from the side of his mouth, taking a mouthful of water.

"It was very good thank you. Worth every penny."

"You know James, this has been very enjoyable. I don't suppose you'd like to continue this conversation sometime?" She asked hopefully.

"I'd love to Alice. I know you have to go back to work, so when would you like to do this again?"

"I realize that this may sound too quick, but do you have plans for tonight?"

"No, not at all. Would you like to go out for a meal?"

"Why don't you come over to my place when I finish work? I'll rustle up something if that's okay with you. No pressure, just an informal meal. Not a date or anything."

James could see the sincerity in her face and agreed, asking for her address and the time to show up.

When they went their separate ways after lunch, they both felt a spring in their step and looking forward to spending more time together.

While Alice returned to work, James went home to his computer, his eyes riveted to the screen until he got ready to go over to Alice's. He freshened up but only changed his shirt, choosing a light blue dress shirt that he kept unbuttoned at the neck.

He stopped on the way over to pick up a bottle of wine, selecting a Californian merlot that he was fond of.

Alice's apartment was practically in the center of Palo Alto. Within yards she could dine at a number of fine restaurants or shop the upscale stores. It was a very vibrant neighborhood, but a place you felt safe in no matter what the hour.

Her apartment wasn't huge, but very befitting a single professional woman. Most of it was open, with the living space, kitchen, and small dining area enclosed within it. The only doors were for the bedroom, guest bathroom, and closets. She had hardwood floors with a large rug in the living space, and her overstuffed couch and one armchair faced the fake gas fire and fireplace. She had a flat screen TV above the mantel, and a glass coffee table on the rug, covered with magazines. The walls were pastel colored and the furniture dark brown. She had family pictures everywhere, but also a couple of seascape watercolors. There were no drapes on the windows, just cream wooden blinds, and her dining table was glass, matching the coffee table in design.

When James entered the apartment after Alice buzzed him in, he liked her décor, but he loved her kitchen. He still liked to cook, so he was very impressed with the six burner gas stove, the large double oven, a big island, and excellent cookware. She also had a double door refrigerator and a walk in larder. Even the sink was large with plenty of room to wash the pans, and to rinse them off and drain. Virtually everything was in fingerprint proof stainless steel, and with the pans hanging over the island, everything was to hand.

Alice hadn't been home long before James arrived as she'd been kept late at work. She'd managed to pick up a French loaf and had quickly changed into jeans and a white v necked tee shirt. She'd just unpinned her hair when the doorbell rang, and was very apologetic when James entered.

She explained what had happened at work and said they could go out, but if he was game, then she could do a quick spaghetti dish. James told her that pasta would be good and that he'd be happy to help, so Alice poured them both a glass of wine and they went to work.

Alice got the salad ingredients out of the fridge along with a bowl and had James put it together. She put a large pot of water on the stove, and while it was heating she began to brown the minced beef that she had, and started throwing in ingredients, along with a bottle of pasta sauce once it was browned. James, having finished the salad bowl, offered to do some garlic bread, and very quickly he made a paste of garlic, butter and parmesan, which he spread onto the cut loaf. As Alice threw spaghetti in the now boiling water, James turned on the broiler and put the bread on a foil lined baking sheet.

Everything came together all at the same time, and they served themselves from the pans once the pasta was drained and returned, taking their plates to the small table, along with their wine. It certainly wasn't what Alice had planned that afternoon, but it had worked, and she had felt comfortable around James.

They talked with ease all evening. James helped with the cleaning up, and while he had coffee sitting on the couch, Alice stayed on the wine as she sat on the armchair. They talked about everything. If felt good for them to hear that someone else had encountered similar problems to their own, so both were more open than they'd ever been.

The evening didn't develop romantically, neither pushed it, but they both felt a spark that they wanted to pursue.

James didn't try to kiss Alice as he made to leave, but he did ask her if he could see her again, and Alice readily agreed. As he turned to say so long to her at the front door, he was very pleased when she gave him a quick kiss on the cheek.

He promised he would call her the following day, and she gave him a final hug to say goodnight.

CHAPTER 13

James did call Alice the following day. He told her how much he'd enjoyed being with her, and that he wanted to take her out at the weekend. Have dinner and go to the movies maybe. Alice said that would be great, but sounded a little disappointed that they couldn't do that sooner.

James would have loved to have seen her before then, but he had work to do on and away from the computer with Teco Gervasini and Jonathon White.

Jonathon lived a humdrum life. He'd married after going to community college, was still wedded to her, and father of a boy and girl who were both in Elementary School. His wife, Julie, had returned to the workplace and was earning good money as a personal assistant. It was perfect for her as she could do most of the work from home.

Julie had gotten her figure back now, was still very attractive, although her husband had developed a bit of a paunch. He still retained his blonde hair that he kept at shoulder length, but now sported a mustache as well. He kept his chin shaved, but his sideburns came down to below his ears. He looked like an overweight surfer.

Jonathon still liked to steal, but nothing much from what James could determine. He surmised that Jonathon passed it of as store theft, then sold the games without ringing them up.

He didn't do much of interest, just went straight to work in the mornings after sometimes dropping off the kids, then went directly home from the store. He did employ a young lad at minimum wage, and the kid generally closed up the store and set the alarm.

Jonathon and Julie would sometimes take the children out for dinner, but all Jonathon had to himself was a regular round of golf on Sunday morning with three of his high school friends. James knew them by sight, but they had always been the audience for Jonathon.

Using a prepaid phone, James called Jonathon at his store.

"Peninsula Video Games. How may I help you?" Jonathon answered, matter of factly.

"Is this Mr. White I'm speaking to?" Asked James.

"Yes, it is. Is there something I can help you with?"

"I have a proposition for you Mr. White. Would you be interested?"

"If this is a sales call then no. Is there anything further you need to ask?"

"I have all the latest video games Mr. White, in all formats. Nintendo, Play Station, Wii, Mac, Xbox, whatever you want. I can let you have them for 10% of the retail value, so if I have a hundred thousand dollars worth, they're yours for ten. Are you interested?"

"Who is this? Who am I talking to? Is this some kind of set up?" Jonathan didn't wait for a reply as he continued. "I already have a supplier, the company I work for. I don't want, nor can I have, another supplier. You'll need to call someone else."

"As you wish Mr. White. I only called you because a friend of mine bought a new game from you for half price. I was under the impression that you liked to make some money for yourself rather than your supplier. Obviously, I've made a mistake and I will go elsewhere. Goodbye Mr. White, I'm sorry I've wasted your time."

"Who are you?" Asked Jonathon, before James could hang up.

"You can call me Mr. Smith if you like. I'm just looking to do a little business Mr. White, that's all. I make money, and the people I sell to make money. We just cut out the middle men. I made a mistake calling you so now I will go. Goodbye Mr. White."

"Are you the police or something?" Enquired Jonathon, not sure now what was going on.

"No. I just have very many brand new video games that I need to dispose of and you were recommended. That's okay, I understand where you're coming from so it's no problem. I have other people I can call."

"How many games do you have?" Jonathon was beginning to sound interested.

" I don't know the exact amount. It's a trailer full. I suspect it's in the region of a couple of million dollars worth"

"A trailer? How on earth did you come by a trailer full?" Jonathon asked, not having heard of any big thefts.

"Let's just say Mr. White that I'm a collector. I have several trailers and one of them contains video games. I can dispose of them elsewhere quite easily because I'm not asking for their real worth. I would rather make a quick deal than hang on to them,"

"This is a wind up Mr. Smith, or whatever you're called. You're just trying to set me up."

"I won't waste any more of your time Mr. White. I can tell you're not interested. Have a good day."

"Wait a second. Can we meet in person?" Jonathon pleaded.

"Not a good idea Mr. White. I don't meet anyone I do business with, it's safer that way for all concerned. I use prepaid phones that I change regularly, and any transactions are done by wire."

"I couldn't take a trailer full."

"That would be up to you. The more you take, the more profit there is for you. If you can't afford a full trailer then I can add another buyer. The trailer isn't going anywhere, it's safe and secure. Two buyers are okay but no more. That's too risky Mr. White. To show you I'm on the level with you, I'll send you some games in a day or two. I will then call you back and see what you want to do. Anything less than half the trailer I go elsewhere. If in the meantime someone wants the whole trailer, you won't hear from me again. Okay?"

"Okay," replied Jonathon, his mind racing as the call ended and he thought of the profit from a half trailer full of new video games, and how he could raise the money to buy it.

James had been searching on the computer while he talked and now needed to go out in his car. He was already dressed, but he took out a small overnight case from a closet, checking the contents before leaving.

Teco Gervasini was now a legal bully in a cop uniform. He was already on to his third wife, and now his sixth partner as a police officer.

James had been able to garner some information about him, but it wasn't good reading. He'd been reported many times for over excessive behavior. His second wife had a restraining order against him. Neighbors had complained about him. It seemed no one liked working with him. A reporter had been asking, to anyone who would listen, why he was still able to work for the police department.

Although Teco didn't have any children living with him and his present wife, he did have a young son who lived with Teco's second wife, his mother. His current spouse always looked dowdy to James, who suspected that beneath her unflattering appearance, that she was quite good looking. James thought Teco didn't want her to look attractive to other men, and he was sure that he beat her. She always seemed to be hurting.

James wanted to get Teco on film, beating one of his victims, but he knew it was going to be difficult. With the patrol cars having cameras now on their dashboards, it was hard for Teco to pull someone over and then hit them. He had to be sneaky about it and make sure a complaint wouldn't be made.

James realized he needed to dig deeper.

Teco and his wife lived on Carlos Avenue in Redwood City, in a three level townhouse. Directly across the street was a motel, which was perfect for James's purpose.

After checking in under his real name, James unpacked his overnight bag. It didn't contain any clothes, just another laptop, a wireless receiver, a USB adapter, and tiny wireless cameras with motion detectors and audio.

They had cost James a pretty penny, but now he was going to get good use out of them.

He called Teco's house to make sure his wife wasn't home. He knew Teco was at work, and thought he knew where the wife was, but needed to be sure. He called twice and both times it went to voicemail, which he ignored, and as he'd used a prepaid phone he wasn't concerned.

Placing the cameras in a small bag and putting on a floppy sun hat, James made his way across the street and rang the doorbell, at the same time pulling out his door opening kit. There was no answer, and seeing no one around he quickly opened the door.

The alarm hadn't been set which was helpful, so James left the door on the latch, then finding the door that led down to the garage, he went down the stairs to verify it was empty. Returning, he left the door open so he could hear the garage door if Teco's wife came home.

The first floor consisted of a living room that led to the dining room and kitchen at the back. James quickly hid two of the cameras that would capture all three rooms, checking from all sides that they couldn't be seen. They were only the size of a dime, yet the picture and audio quality were amazing. He then hurried upstairs. The room on the right was spare, so entering the master bedroom he found the perfect places for his cameras and hid them there. He went back downstairs, closed the door to the basement, and left the way he had entered, making sure the door was locked behind him. He was in and out within five minutes.

When he got back to the motel he set up the laptop and checked the pictures. They were perfect. Anywhere within two hundred feet these cameras worked like a dream. James had it all set up to record all motion, and after he disturbed the bed to make it looked slept in, he left the motel.

James then went home to call an old acquaintance.

James's old friend was called Wesley, and he knew him from helping him to gain access to various places, in return for being kept safe in the poor neighborhood of Redwood City.

Wesley still had the same number, and when James reminded him who he was, he sounded happy to hear from him.

"Yo, James, been a long time man. What you been up to dude?"

"Not a lot Wesley, but I may be able to put something your way if you're interested. How are you anyway?"

"I'm good James, still trying to make a dollar here and there. So what you got for me?"

Despite it being a few years now since James had done anything for him, Wesley still trusted him, as James had never let him down.

"A good payday in return for a couple of favors."

"What favors do you need James? You know I owe you."

"Firstly, there's some information I need Wesley. Do you know of a cop called Teco Gervasini?"

"He's a son of a bitch James, stay well clear. He's a nasty bastard. What the hell do you want from him?"

"I just want to give him his comeuppance, that's all. Do you have anything on him?"

"Only that it's best to keep away. If he wasn't a cop he'd be in the ground by now. He gives regular beatings to some guys I know, even though they give him money to leave them alone. He just likes to beat on folk, whether they pay him or not."

"Where does this happen Wesley? I think I may have a solution to this problem."

"Just be careful James. Real careful. I'll make a call to see what the routine is, but this cop hits first and then asks questions. So what's the payday?"

"Half of a trailer full of brand new video games to do with as you wish, and I'll reimburse you for the other half. I'll need someone to drive a tractor trailer, which I'll get him into and start, then he will need to drive it to an empty warehouse, if you can find one. In the warehouse, I'll need half the trailer emptied into another one, then he can drive your half away."

"I think I can arrange that James. When do you want this to happen?"

"Whenever you can. If you get an offshore bank account I will transfer the money there once it's done."

"You don't seem to be getting much in return James. You sure about this?"

"You've been a good friend Wesley and I appreciate that. This is a small thank you. What I'll get out of it is priceless. So what else do you know about our bad cop?"

Wesley told him what he knew and took down James's number so he could call when he knew more. He also told him to be extremely wary.

CHAPTER 14

It was three days before James got what he wanted from Teco's house, and it was just as he suspected. Teco's wife was being abused, and it was very disturbing to view. Teco especially liked to hit her on various parts of her body so it wouldn't be seen by others, and it could be anything to set him off. A look, a meal he didn't like, or even her not moving quickly enough when told to get him a beer. In the bedroom it was worse.

Once the house was empty, he retrieved his cameras and checked out of the motel. He was on his way home when Wesley called, to say he had everything in place for the trailer, and to call back when he wanted to do it. He also relayed the routine that Teco employed to garner his illicit money.

That night, James took Alice to the Levanda Restaurant, and then to see the Best Exotic Marigold Hotel at the movie theater in Palo Alto.

The restaurant was Californian with an Italian flair and very good, the movie was a typical British comedy drama with a cast full of aging stars, and they both enjoyed the food, the film, and each other.

They felt very comfortable with each other and talked about their insecurities with their looks. Both had problems still with self confidence, but to hear each other admit that, was very beneficial to them.

They also talked about bullying.

Alice had never thought she was being bullied until being hit one day at high school. It was only later that she realized that bullying took on many forms and that a beating could sometimes be more welcome. When she compared notes with James, she was grateful that she'd never been forced to do other kids work for them, or had all her money taken all the time. Alice couldn't even say hello to anyone without them having to endure a dose of her treatment, so she became even more isolated.

James hated always being blamed for everything, his books being ripped up, and the name calling. For some reason, the name calling always got to him more than having his bones broken, especially when it was about his mom.

Neither of them thought the teachers had helped any, which they didn't understand. Protecting the jocks was almost normal for schools, but insofar that they let them get away with so much, was dismaying to James and Alice. They'd been victimized for being weaker or different, and thousands of other kids were going through exactly the same thing every day.

They both discussed their self confidence issues, and agreed that they'd mostly been able to eliminate them. Except for their appearance. They still appeared to themselves as weak and unattractive, not even normal. Especially Alice.

Discussing the relationships they'd had, James's fling with Trudy was the longest that either of them had, which at their age was ridiculous.

Alice mentioned that having someone stay the night was her biggest nightmare, as she thought she was especially horrid in the mornings, in the light, and didn't want to be seen then. So invariably she had one night stands, ushering her partner out of the door before dawn to avoid that.

James's problem was normal dating. He'd never really done it since being at the locksmith's, and as that hadn't ended well, he was still very wary. He wanted to change, but it was difficult.

Alice asked him if he thought he would ever expel his demons from school. James told her he was slowly working on it and so far it was going well. There were just a few more steps to do, and then most of his bad memories wouldn't haunt him so much.

James asked Alice if there was someone from high school that she had bad feelings toward.

Alice's only thought from high school was the principal. Her parents had complained to him on a number of occasions, but he had done nothing. Her brother was now at the school, but as he was on the football team he was mainly left alone, but he was still picked on for his red hair. Yet the principal still did nothing. Alice didn't like the girls who had persecuted her, but she felt she had gained her revenge on them by having her career.

When getting the question back, James agreed with Alice about the principal, but also about another teacher, who when seeing James being dunked head first into a non flushed toilet, just told the boys holding his feet not to injure him or make too much noise. The same teacher had also seen James being badly beaten up once. He had never even attempted to stop it.

Alice asked James if he could ever forgive them. He replied that in most cases, if anyone did him wrong but then apologized he could accept it. When it came to the two teachers, he couldn't, as they were the adults in charge and knew better.

After the movie was over they walked hand in hand back to Alice's apartment. They were both in jeans and tee shirts although Alice's fit her figure way better than James's. They'd snuggled together in the theater as it had been chilly in there, and James had liked the way she smelt and felt against him.

Alice invited James up for a nightcap and he accepted, following her into the kitchen as she went to get a bottle of wine. As she turned around to show him the bottle, he kissed her, and was mightily relieved when she kissed him back, still clutching the wine over his shoulder.

She asked him to stay the night. James told her that he would stay, but not for the night. He would only stay overnight when she was comfortable enough to take a shower with him, and not in the dark. With all the lights on, or in daylight.

She agreed, put down the wine and led him into her dark bedroom.

When she woke up in the early morning daylight, she was sorry he wasn't still there. She still had a tingling and a warmth between her legs that felt really good. She was even still naked beneath the sheet. Seeing a note on her nightstand she read it while still lying on her back, and she smiled when she read it.

"Will call you later. Can't wait to see you again, and last night was wonderful. P.S. You have a fabulous body and a beautiful face. Let me know about the shower. Love James xx"

Alice already knew that James wasn't a one night stand for her, she definitely wanted to see him again.

CHAPTER 15

James went to the library's computer to do more research. He already knew where the video game company's distribution center was, he now needed to find out the truck schedules. The distribution center opened at 5am, but it closed at 3pm. Any trailer that arrived around that time wouldn't be unloaded until first thing in the morning.

Virtually everyone kept track of their delivery trucks these days, with GPS trackers it was like having a spy in every cab. This company was no exception. Having little trouble getting into the system, James soon had a nationwide map of where all their trucks were, and there was one truck with a full load, which had an ETA of 2:30pm. It would just have enough time to back up to the unloading bay.

Staying on the system, James also found out that the alarm for the distribution center and the yard could be set by either a computer or cell phone, providing it was connected to the internet. All you needed to do was download a free app. The only thing James required was the code and he had it and tested it within five minutes. He was good to go.

After deleting all trace of his actions on the public computer, James left the library and called Wesley, asking how soon they could go.

"Whenever Man, my guys are just hangin around chillin. You wanna go tonight?"

"No. How about in a couple of hours Wesley?"

"You serious man? In broad daylight?"

"Yes. No one will give it a second thought seeing a tractor trailer in the middle of the afternoon. At night, it's suspicious. It's all set up. If the truck is still attached to the trailer we'll be in and out in 2 minutes. If it's unhooked, then it will be five. No one will even notice."

"Let me ask my guys dude."

Wesley went quiet for three to four minutes before coming back on the line.

"Okay man, we're good. I trust you dude. Where do you need to go to?"

"Livermore. It's a distribution center in a very quiet area. The only thing nearby is another center, and a hotel where the truckers probably stay. The center closes down at three, so if I delay the alarm for a couple of minutes no one will notice."

"The guys will pick you up at one o'clock. Traylon and Kirk they're called. Tell me somewhere near your home they can pick you up."

James did so, and asked for them to bring false plates for the tractor trailer before he hung up the phone.

After talking to Wesley, James called Alice who answered on the first ring. She wanted him to go over for dinner, but he could arrive sooner if he wished. James said he'd be over for dinner, but that he had something to take care of first. Alice said she'd had a wonderful night and had missed him on waking up. James was smiling broadly as he said goodbye, knowing he wasn't going to be another of her one night stands.

James went home and got his stuff ready. He was taking his spare laptop with a remote broadband connection. His lock tools. A prepaid phone with the app downloaded on to it. His big floppy hat. He rechecked everything before leaving to be picked up.

Traylon and Kirk didn't speak much during the drive to Livermore, possibly wondering what Wesley had got them into with this white dude, leaving James to work on his computer and phone. Kirk was the truck driver, and Traylon was going to drive James and himself back. Both of them were big and mean looking, various tattoos visible on their necks and thick arms. James had never asked Wesley if he was involved with a gang, but Kirk and Traylon did have similar markings on their necks.

They also wore thick gold necklaces, and gold on their fingers and wrists. Kirk was a little shorter than Traylon, his head shaved compared to his friends's patterned cut. They both also sported sleeveless tee shirts, Kirk's black to Traylon's blue. James felt puny compared to his new black partners in crime.

They got to the distribution center early, and James was able to tell them almost to the second when the truck was going to arrive.

As the driver pressed the intercom on the gate whilst still in his cab, James was on the computer, totally concentrated. When the gate slid open he was in control.

They watched from their concealed parking place as the truck swung around in the yard and backed up to the one open bay, someone signaling to the driver as he reversed then stopped. The driver got out of the cab and went to the rear of the trailer, talking to the guy who was holding his hands out wide and shrugging his shoulders.

The driver went back to his truck disconsolately, as the guy closed the bay door, taking a large bag out of the cab and walking away. He didn't unhook the trailer. As he approached the gate it opened, and he walked in the direction of the nearby hotel.

At three o'clock it was a mass exodus, and James was watching his phone intently. Once the last car left and disappeared around the corner, he told Traylon to drive, opening the gate as they approached. Traylon drove over to the truck and James, with his floppy hat on, jumped out of the car. He'd seen the driver lock the truck so he went to work on it, and once he had it open did the same with the ignition. It was idling when Kirk got into the seat, and he was putting it in gear and releasing the brakes when James got back into the car. He and Traylon led the way out, then waited for Kirk to pass them and the gate to close, before James hit the Arm button on his phone.

Kirk and Traylon had replaced the plates and checked the rear doors while James opened the truck, and they took a route that wouldn't pass the driver's hotel. They had been in and out within three minutes.

Following Kirk, Traylon kept a keen eye on the mirrors and they both stayed at the speed limit, James erasing all his links to the distribution center and dismantling the phone. Seeing they were heading towards the tiny airport in Redwood City after over an hour of driving, James asked where the warehouse was.

"Change of plan man. Wes has this hangar that's cool. We'll be there in a second."

James let it be. He didn't care, but he was curious.

They followed the trailer into the open hanger and the doors were immediately closed behind them. Kirk parked next to an empty trailer and Wesley appeared with other guys, and a fork lift truck.

As James and Traylon got out of the car, Wesley came to greet them but Traylon spoke first.

"You need to hire this guy boss, that was so fuckin easy"

"So, no problems?" asked Wesley, shaking their hands.

"It was so damn quick, I can't even remember what happened" added Traylon.

"Man, I've missed you James." Greeted Wesley with a smile and a hug, " I'd almost forgotten how friggin good you are. Look at you now! No glasses, no skinny body, you look good man! Come on, let's see what's in the trailer."

Wesley was a big man as well. Huge really in both height and body, but not fat. More of a body builder who still lifted weights, but not as much as he probably used to do.

Just as James remembered him, Wesley still liked to wear Hawaiian shirts over his pants. His head was as smooth as a billiard ball, features pockmarked with various scars, tattoos on his neck and arms, bling like Traylon and Kirk, and a warm smile that revealed three random gold teeth.

They walked over happily to the trailer which was now open, and they were hauling out pallets with clear plastic enveloping the boxes of games. Wesley's guys were putting the pallets into the empty trailer, but also putting boxes into three box trucks that Wesley had brought.

"I didn't expect to see you here Wesley," said James surprised.

"Normally I wouldn't. I just had to see this. Kirk called me from the truck and said how simple it had been, so I came down for a look. He's taken a shine to the truck. Do you need it for anything?" Asked Wesley.

"Nope. I just don't want it coming back to me."

"No worries there James. Kirk knows what happens if he starts chatting." Wesley's tone indicated the dire consequences of such a thing.

"Then give him an early Christmas present."

"What about the stuff we're leaving James?" Asked Wesley.

"I'll see about that, but consider it sold Wesley. I do need to take some of the games with me"

"You're the man James. I now owe you big time. Anything you ever need, just call. Okay? We'll send some of the stuff with you"

"Okay Wesley. There are no ties to you with this place?"

"None at all. If your buyer brings the pigs they'll get nowhere. We'll leave the side door open for you, not that you need it, but you know what I mean."

"I know. It's good seeing you again Wesley."

"You too James. Traylon will take you home now but call me anytime, you hear?"

"I hear. Take care of yourself."

Wesley had never mentioned it to James, but when all the sirens had converged on the neighborhood when James's mom was killed, Wesley had gone to see what all the fuss was about. Wesley saw her on the hood of the truck, and when they pulled the truck away he witnessed her lower body falling away.

Wesley was a tough man, he'd been in fights, been shot at and knifed, but seeing that had made him gag. It had been awful. Wesley had no time for cops, but that night they did the right thing in stopping James from going down to the scene.

Wesley knew that James and his mom had moved in to his neighborhood, but didn't know them at the time to speak to. He resolved to keep an eye on James after the accident, but after learning that James was also a whizz with locks, he used his talents occasionally, then made it known that James was in his crew. If anyone hurt him, they would have himself personally to deal with.

Getting home, James had just enough time to put the games in his car trunk, shower and change, before heading over to Alice's. He was famished by the time he got there, not to mention exhausted, but she made him feel really welcome.

It was almost dawn when he woke up, and he seriously thought about going back to sleep. He wrote another note and left for his own bed.

CHAPTER 16

Alice woke up to a lonely bed again and another note.

"You're a great cook and a better lover. Sorry I was too tired for seconds. I didn't want to leave again this morning but will call you later. Love James xx"

Alice lay back on the pillows and could smell James and her own scent intermingled. Again, she was still naked which was so unusual for her. Normally after sex, she immediately put on some clothing, be it a shirt, sleepwear, or her underwear.

The window shutters were keeping the room in a low light, but as she got up she ignored the clothing that James had frantically removed from her last night. She walked up to the full length mirror and looked at herself. She thought she was far from perfect, but looking again she liked the way her legs appeared. Long, slender, and no cellulite yet. Her hips seemed big, but seemed to give her a good shape. The breasts were firm and not sagging. Turning around and looking over her shoulder, she thought her ass was a bit droopy, not as pert or shaped as she would have preferred. She gave it a wiggle and laughed at her reflection. All in all, she didn't think she looked as bad as she thought. She stayed in front of the mirror looking at herself from all angles, as she strove to feel confident in her nudity.

James woke up a little later. He was hungry again, and walking around his apartment in just his boxer shorts, he got some coffee made and threw some eggs in a mixing bowl. Sipping the coffee, he scrambled the eggs and put some bread in the toaster, taking the eggs off the heat before they were fully cooked and buttered the toast.

Putting everything on a plate, he sat at the kitchen counter, added some steak sauce to the eggs, and turned on his laptop as he ate.

He didn't expect to see any news of the video games theft and nor did he, but he did find a small item about Tommy Hilditch. It had been quite a while since he'd left him in the lions enclosure. Upon reading it though, it was just an update of sorts. "The former pupil of Woodside High School, Tommy Hilditch, was finally laid to rest last week. The police spokesman in Fresno said they were still treating the case as a tragic accident. You may remember that Mr. Hilditch was found fatally mutilated in a mountain lion's enclosure, and that the Fresno Police had found him in the unlocked cage with a knife and a loaded rifle. His truck was also on the scene with the keys still in the ignition. The police think Mr. Hilditch went to kill the lions for trophy sport, but that one of the two lions caught him unawares when he inexplicably entered the enclosure and was closing the door behind him. Mr. Hilditch is survived by his loving wife and two children."

Noting the time, James got up and put his dishes in the dishwasher and refilled his coffee. He then took his drink to the bathroom, where he shaved and brushed his teeth. He then took a hot shower.

After he toweled himself dry and did his grooming, he got dressed very casually in white shorts, and a white tee shirt with an in-and-out burger house motif. Slipping on some flip flops and picking up his wallet, sunglasses, and car keys, he left the apartment.

The apartments had a huge recycle bin and James found just what he wanted right on the top of it. A good size, empty cardboard box with no address label. He took it over to the trunk of his car, and seeing no one around, he filled it with the games. He didn't have any tape so he just interlocked the flaps on the box closed. The box was too tall for the trunk, so he put it on the back seat and took off. Pulling up at the video store and seeing the street was still quiet, he took out the box and left it on the doorstep. He then drove down the street a little before turning around and parking, so that he could watch the doorway and make sure no-one stole the box. Although none of the stores were open this day, it was too risky to leave a box on a doorstep for very long.

He made a quick call to Jonathon White from a prepaid phone. He told him he'd had a delivery and it was on the store's doorstep.

James didn't see him arrive. The tenants of the stores had back entrances with parking, so that's how they entered. Within five minutes of the call, James watched as Jonathon opened the front door, and took a look around before carrying the box inside. James drove away.

James was still hungry, and although he liked to eat healthily most of the time, sometimes it just didn't sate him. He went home via Round Table Pizza, where he picked up a barbecued chicken pizza.

After eating most of the pizza, he called Alice who wanted him to go over. He'd survived her two night limit. As much as he wanted to, he was aware now that his actions with his tormentors could affect Alice. He knew he really liked her and he didn't want her to get hurt in any way. He'd never thought for one moment that he would meet someone when he'd started this, and if he'd gotten caught then so be it. It would have been worth it. He still wanted, and needed, to finish his list, but now he had a reason to avoid prison. He was changing his future plans purely because of Alice.

Alice tried to entice him over. James didn't think she was, but she told him that she was naked beneath her dress, and that if he went over for dinner she would cook with just an apron on. He could even keep the lights on when they went to bed, if they made it that far.

James was aware that he was disappointing her, but he resisted her charms and told her he really needed to work for the rest of the day. That was difficult to explain as she knew he did very little. He got around it by saying his shares needed sorting out before the Hong Kong Stock exchange opened. Not a total lie, but his shares were fine.

He made the call better by asking her to call the next day, and that perhaps they could spend a hot weekend somewhere, which he would arrange.

CHAPTER 17

James gave Wesley a call to get his offshore bank account number. Wesley had obtained one, but thought it might be traceable as he didn't have the skills needed to prevent that. James assured him that he would deal with it, and that by the time the money arrived in his account, it would be untraceable.

Wesley reiterated his belief that he owed James 'bigtime." James mentioned to him that he may need help with a special project. It would only take an hour, and that it would be fun. He just needed someone who could operate a septic tank truck, and a kid at Woodside High School who'd be game for a laugh, and to be able to keep his mouth shut. Wesley said it wouldn't be a problem, he knew quite a few kids there. If Kirk couldn't operate the truck, then he knew someone else who would be able to.

Asking James when this would happen, James replied that it would hopefully be in a couple of days, and that he would know for sure once he rechecked the schedules again. He promised to call when he had it confirmed.

Having Wesley's bank details, he then called Jonathon White from the same prepaid phone as before. Jonathon hadn't had a sudden change of heart, he still had the same mentality as when he was at school. He just didn't want to get caught. James told him that he had half a trailer waiting to be emptied, and that he needed the payment for it. Jonathon asked about the other half, so James asked him, knowing the answer, whether he had the money for a full trailer. Jonathon replied that he didn't, but if James could wait a couple of weeks then he would be able to come up with more money. James told Jonathon that he needed the trailer emptied a.s.a.p. and that the other half was already gone. When the money was deposited, he would tell him where the trailer was.

Although he had never mentioned this before, Jonathon now wanted to do a deposit and then pay the balance once he had it all. James smiled. He gave him the bank account number and told him to put 50% of the $100,000 into it within an hour. He would then tell him where the trailer was, and he would expect the balance when he drove the goods away. He also warned Jonathon, that he knew who he was, where he lived, and where he worked. If he started getting cute with this deal of a lifetime, then there'd be serious repercussions.

Jonathon suggested again that they should meet in person, so that he could see who he was dealing with. James told him that wasn't possible, he'd been told that before, and it would leave him open to being compromised as Jonathon already knew him. James suspected that Jonathon wanted to ambush him with his golf buddies, and then take the games for free.

Jonathon immediately thought that James was a delivery driver. He agreed to transfer the money immediately, and would wait for the return call.

After James hung up, he watched the $50,000 zip around the world on his laptop screen, just as he'd arranged, until it came to rest in Wesley's bank.

James was in his car when he called Jonathon back. He told him where the games could be found and how to get in to the hangar. He also told him that it would be less conspicuous if he emptied the trailer during the day, but that was up to him. He just wanted the balance deposited very quickly.

Among the electronic toys that James had bought was a GPS tracker with a waterproof magnetic cover. If he was connected to the internet he could see exactly where it was, every ten feet, across the whole continent. Attached to a vehicle, he could see what speed it was traveling and where it stopped. Even noting the times. It wasn't a cheap toy, but it was one of James's favorites.

Arriving at the back of Jonathon's store, he pulled up alongside his vehicle and after putting on his floppy hat, he pretended something was wrong with his car by lifting the hood. He then went to his trunk and took out the GPS unit, casually slipping it under Jonathon's vehicle, before fiddling with the wires beneath his hood and then closing the lid.

Jumping back into the driver's seat, he was driving away within two minutes of arriving, and he hadn't seen a soul.

Back at home, he watched the computer screen intermittently as he got ready for his evening assignment.

Teco Gervasini was a man of habit. Every day when he was working, he would drive his Ford 150 truck to the police station and park, if he could, in exactly the same place. When his shift ended, he would drive home and park it outside on the street, as it always seemed he had somewhere to go later.

James thought he only did that to check on his wife, making sure she was where she was supposed to be, and to have dinner. James felt desperately sorry for her.

He was already parked, and waiting further down the street when Teco pulled up and lumbered inside. Although James was equipped to break into the truck, he hadn't heard the telltale beep of the vehicle being locked by the remote control. It didn't matter, he would have been inside within seconds, but as he walked nonchalantly to the driver's door he saw the knob inside the door was in the open position.

Jumping in after making sure there was still no-one around, he attached what looked like a thin, tiny black box to the underside of the passenger sun shield using some Velcro. Making sure it wasn't visible to the driver, he exited the truck and casually walked back to his car.

Once inside, and checking the mirrors for anyone paying any interest to him, he started the car and drove around the corner and parked again. Leaving the engine running, he opened the laptop on the passenger seat and located the instrument he'd left in the truck. The little black box was an infra red camera and voice recorder, and James had positioned it to catch the driver and his side window. It was a little out of place, but it would serve the purpose it was intended for. If James wasn't around, it would record on hearing a voice, but if he was close by, he could override that and record at will.

James knew exactly where Teco was going this evening, and he made his way there to wait for his arrival. Although it was a very dangerous part of the nearby town of East Palo Alto, Wesley had spread the word that he was good, so although he got a few looks, he and his car were left alone.

Teco made this trip every two weeks when he was on the day shift. He always did it alone. This was his personal take, and in return for the cash he received, he kept the dealers informed of any up and coming busts. His take though was progressively getting bigger, and if he didn't get what he demanded, then beatings would take place and arrests made.

It was early evening when Teco's white truck passed James, and pulled alongside the sidewalk further down the street on the left hand side.

James watched closely from his dark vantage point and on his computer screen. He could only see his profile, but that was good enough, as Teco parked and lowered the driver's window, hiding a gun by his right thigh.

Three guys came out of the poorly maintained two story house that Teco had parked at. The front yard was just dirt, and the two chairs that were on either side of the screen door were showing the foam beneath the torn fabric. Rap music could be heard from inside, and the only thing that made this old house distinguishable from all the others in the neighborhood, was the gleaming black Cadillac SUV with tinted windows, parked on the driveway.

Teco shouted at the three men.

"You mother fuckers know the drill. One of you bring me my stuff, the other two stay where I can see you. Now. I don't have all fuckin night."

James's hair on the back of his neck came to attention. He'd heard the voice on the video tapes from his home, and hearing Teco's voice again made him feel nauseous, relating it now to the beating of his poor wife, along with his own memories of it from school.

One of the guys in this very black neighborhood, slouched over to the driver's window, but didn't get too close as he handed over a thick wad of notes. The camera caught it perfectly but it was unclear who the guy was beneath the hood he wore.

"Stay right there while I count it. I don't trust you fuckers and keep those hands where I can see them."

The guy kept quiet as Teco counted the bills, taking his hand away from the gun at his side.

"Okay. Next time I come round I want another two hundred. You hear me?" Teco made sure he was heard.

"C'mon man, you're killing us. We can't afford this." The hooded guy pleaded his case.

"No backchat asshole. I was being kind with you. For talking back to me I now want an extra five hundred. You want another beating shit face?" Teco asked him.

There was no answer.

"Now give me the rest" Teco added.

The hooded guy handed over a clear bag that contained tiny Ziploc packets with white powder visible inside them.

Teco took one out of the bags and carefully opened it, before dipping a finger into the powder, and then tasting it. He closed the bag up and put it back.

"Now go back inside and close the door. I'll be back in a couple of weeks at the same time and I'll expect an extra five hundred. Go on. Get out of my sight."

The hooded guy and his two friends went back inside, probably contemplating how to explain this to whoever they worked for, if indeed they did work for someone else.

James watched as Teco stuffed the money into one of his pockets as he held the gun, watching as the guys went back into the house. He leant toward the camera before putting the truck in drive and driving away.

James followed but not closely. He knew where Teco was going to next, he was going to celebrate at his usual place.

James was worried about this part. He hadn't been before starting the relationship with Alice, and he'd thought seriously about it, but he still had this hidden rage when it came to Teco. He had to get it out of his system.

James parked his car a safe distance away in a restaurant parking lot. He found a dark corner and no one paid him any interest as he opened his trunk and got ready.

Teco's usual place was a strip club in downtown Redwood City. A couple of other cops also frequented the place, so it was largely left alone by law enforcement, unless someone started shooting.

Teco parked behind the club amongst the employees cars, and walked around to the front entrance as James was easily able to find a hiding place for himself and his little bag. Opening the bag, he took out his tools and put a pair of latex gloves on. After making sure no one was around, he very quickly opened the passenger door of Teco's locked truck. After grabbing the tiny camera from the sun visor, he checked out the glove box and found the bags of white powder. James had no doubt it was cocaine but he didn't try it, however, he did take one of the tiny bags and put it in one of his pockets. The gun wasn't there, but the compartment between the seats was locked so he unlocked it, and was happy to find it inside. He removed the bullets then relocked them and the gun in the compartment. Having got what he wanted, he exited the truck and relocked it.

He put the camera in his bag and took out the boxer's face mask and the vest, before taking the bag a safe distance away and hiding it by a trash can, that was on his route out. He put the mask and vest on, then went back to his hiding place to wait for Teco.

Teco emerged after about an hour, from the rear door with what looked like one of the stripper's in tow. She was very striking and was in great shape. She looked like she was ready to go back on stage, as she was dressed like a schoolgirl, her blonde long hair hanging loose over the open white blouse that exposed her white bra, her breasts spilling over it. Her plaid skirt was so short you could see her white crutch, her eyes were very dark, and her lips a vivid red.

Teco went directly to the passenger door of his truck, opened it, and leant back against the seat as he fished about in the glove compartment. James heard them talk but couldn't tell what they were saying, but Teco was holding one of the tiny bags aloft.

She looked around and then unbuttoned his pants, pulling them and his underpants down before she squatted and went down on him.

James was ever so grateful he couldn't see everything, but he heard Teco moan and gasp, then saw him hand over the package as she stood up again. As she headed back inside, Teco pulled his pants back up, and when he turned around to close the door James was behind him.

James hit him in the lower back with such force that Teco fell backwards on to the concrete. James didn't relent. He hit him with his hands and his feet and Teco never got a shot in. The face guard and vest were redundant as James pummeled him. The beating was so brutal that Teco never even had chance to yell for help, and was unconscious when James did his worst.

Teco had put most of the money in a bank deposit envelope, which James knew was his secret account. James left it in the truck once he was finished with him, putting some of the coke he'd taken around Teco's nostrils, and the rest into his shirt pocket. He was just leaving when the rear door opened and another woman stepped out. He heard her scream for help as he darted away, totally unseen.

CHAPTER 18

James didn't sleep much that night, he'd scared himself with the ferocity of his blows. He did though feel relieved, like a huge boulder had been lifted off his shoulders. He also knew that Teco would find it hard to ever again beat someone up like he used to do, which was what James wanted to accomplish. If someone came up with proof that James had done it, he would quite happily go to jail. He felt it was worth it, even with Alice now in the picture.

James sent all his video tapes to the reporter who had been investigating Teco. He thought the reporter would prevent the police from protecting one of their own, even though he wasn't liked.

James did feel bad about Teco's wife, but at least now her body would heal and she wouldn't be in fear every day. He'd keep an eye on her and make sure she would have ample funds to do as she wished. Nobody deserved the abuse that he'd witnessed her receiving.

James called Alice and asked if she was okay for the weekend away. He thought they could go to Half Moon Bay. When she asked what they would do there, he replied that they could eat, drink, but mainly stay in bed for the weekend. Alice thought that sounded great and couldn't wait.

She then asked if he'd heard the news. It seemed that someone they went to school with, Teco Gervasini, was severely beaten up. He'd had limbs broken in multiple places, and the police suspected that some drug dealers had done it. Although Teco was a cop, they were also investigating some evidence found at the scene, along with other breaking developments, that could possibly explain everything. Apparently, there was a lot more to the story.

James replied that he'd heard that he was a bent cop, who was on the take from some drug dealers, and that he wasn't very well liked around town.

Alice said she knew he was nasty in school, and that what goes around, comes around. As Alice had left the door ajar with that comment, James quickly asked her if anything really bad had happened to her at school or college. When he'd asked before, it seemed to James that she was holding something back from him.

It took a while for her to answer, he'd obviously hit a very exposed nerve.

"You know James" she began, "I've never talked about this to anyone. I think my family have a good idea of what I went through, but I didn't tell them all of it as I knew they would have created a fuss, and it would probably have made things worse for me."

"I can understand that Alice, I thought the same way."

"This is hard James, but I think I need to finally get it out of my system. It's just been stagnating inside of me, so let me tell you about it."

James kept quiet.

"I thought school was bad, you know, with the tripping up, the showers, the chewing gum in my hair, and being made to fight. The showers especially I dreaded. With being slow to develop the other girls would call me a boy, make fun of my red hair and freckles, and tell me I was a freak because my breasts weren't growing. They would say that I would end up a bitter spinster, as no boy would ever look at me or ask me out, as I was just too ugly for anyone. It was horrible, and I would come up with wild excuses to try to get out of any of the sports, just so I didn't have to shower. All sorts of things were thrown at me, I was beaten up, and then when I got my first period I didn't live it down for ages. They called me the bleeding carrot. God, I hated school. Then I had my first year at college."

Alice began to cry softly as she recalled her first year, her voice intermittently breaking up as she related to James what had happened.

"I didn't want to join any sororities at college, I just wanted to be left alone to do my studying. I thought I'd have to go through a hazing, or do drugs, and I wasn't interested in partying either.

It didn't make much difference. The president of one of the sorority's, Susan Ward she was called, was in her senior year, and for some reason took a liking to me, but not in a good way. It was all bad.

At first it was quite flattering. I was slowly beginning to physically develop, and I was gradually getting my hair and skin under control, so receiving compliments from Susan after all the abuse at school was welcoming. She was a beautiful girl, tall, long straight black hair, powerful with being a president, and she had everyone under her spell. Getting praise from her made others curb their tongues. Not all of them, but some at least.

I naively thought that she only wanted me in her house because I had more of a brain than the others, but I was wrong. Very wrong. She wanted me sexually"

There was another pause as Alice gathered herself, before she finally continued.

"Susan came to my room one night and told my roommate to disappear. My roommate was a tiny Japanese girl who totally kept to herself. She barely even spoke to me. She practically ran from the room when Susan spoke to her. I wasn't that concerned, not until Susan locked the door and began to undress, telling me to do the same. I had no idea why she wanted me to do this, I was still very innocent and had never had sex with anyone, so I asked her why. She said she wanted us to make out. By this time, she was down to this black leather basque and getting closer to me. I'd been lying on top of my bed in my flannel pajamas studying, and as I stood up she pushed me back down. She was way stronger than me. I tried to fight back, but I just didn't have the strength. Before I knew it, she had torn off my top and pants, I was naked, and she was raping me. She'd brought a vibrator with her to use on me. Then holding my hair, she forced me to go down on her, and if I slapped her, or yelled for help, it just made her more intense. I didn't know it at the time, but she was into S and M. She raped me James!" Alice sobbed.

"I am so sorry Alice. I can't even imagine your pain. That is awful."

"It didn't stop there James. She would come to my room every few days and she would bring whips and canes. If she didn't think they hurt me enough, then she'd bite and scratch me, penetrate me with a dildo. I just didn't have the strength to fight her off, and if I tried, she'd hit me even harder. I can still feel the welts on my body where I was struck, and to this day I feel ashamed, even after all this time. Can you forgive me James?" Alice pleaded.

"You were the victim Alice. You must understand that. It wasn't your fault. It's like saying a kid deserves to be beaten up because he's not as good looking as everyone else."

"I know James. It's just that sometimes it gets to a point where you begin to think it was your own fault."

"That is very true Alice, I've had those thoughts myself. What happened to this Susan? Did you report it and get her expelled?"

"I couldn't. Like I said, she was very popular and powerful, and if I had, it may have even gotten worse. I just waited for her to go."

"Was she doing medicine like yourself?"

"No. She was doing a business degree. I've never seen her since she left, thank god, but I heard she was some bigwig in New York by the time I graduated. At least my other years at college were very quiet after that. I would probably have killed myself, or someone else if it had continued. I'm sorry James, I should have told you all this sooner. Do you think you'll still be able to look at me?"

"Of course Alice. I feel quite humbled and honored that you told me all this. I know it was far from easy for you, but I hope you'll feel some relief from doing so."

"I do James. I'm going to have to get back to work now, but do you think you could come over tonight? I could really do with a big hug right now."

"I'll come over and I'll bring a carry out from somewhere. Will 7 o'clock be okay?"

"Yes, and thank you. It will give me time to get cleaned up after all these tears. So I'll see you later?"

"Yes, Alice, I'll see you later. We'll have a good night."

CHAPTER 19

James was very saddened after talking to Alice. He thought he'd had it bad but at least he hadn't been raped. He had no idea how he would have handled that, and for it to have happened multiple times, truly appalled him.

When he eventually opened his laptop he had calmed down somewhat, but he was annoyed to discover that Jonathon White had still to deposit the balance for his video games.

Calling him, Jonathon was obviously stalling, saying he had no more room and that it was taking longer than he thought to empty the trailer. He wanted extra time to remove the games, but that he would be done soon, he could be trusted.

James was in no mood to be misinformed. He told Jonathon that the trailer had to be emptied by first thing in the morning as the hangar's lease was up. The longer that Jonathon took to take his goods, the more likelihood they'd be caught. The money had to be deposited today. James informed Jonathon that if he didn't wire the money within two hours, then he would have no choice but to inform the thieves who the buyer was, and they were not the type of people to mess with.

Jonathon pleaded with James not to mention his name, but James told him he had no other option, and he certainly wasn't going to take a severe beating for him. James told Jonathon that he thought the thieves could well have been behind the beating of the cop in East Palo Alto, that it certainly sounded like them. He was sure as hell he wasn't going to give excuses for him.

The money was wired within minutes.

James checked the GPS unit and saw that Jonathon had made a couple of visits to a storage location. He resolved to go there later, and hopefully find out which unit it was. In the meantime, he watched the money move around the globe until it nestled in Wesley's account.

He then went to the Woodside High School website, and after a few clicks and some typing, found the teacher's schedule. Mr. Long was doing the lunch time yard monitoring the following day.

Sean Long had been a teacher at Woodside for many years, but was still fairly new when James had been attending.

At that time, James knew that many of the girls had a crush on him as he was fairly young, but mainly because he was good looking. He had a certain resemblance to the departed movie actor James Dean, and although you'd have been hard pressed to find one of the girls who had even heard of James Dean, he was very striking.

Although James thought that Mr. Long may very well have had sex with several of the girls, he wasn't upset with him for that, nor did he want to go down that particular road. James's beef was that Mr. Long had personally witnessed him being bullied on more than one occasion, yet had totally ignored it, even when he got his arm broken by Teco Gervasini.

The worst example in James's view, had been when Tommy Hilditch and some of his friends had attacked James in the bathroom. James had nothing to give them, so they first beat him up, and then followed that up by putting him head first into a toilet that someone had just dumped in.

Mr Long had stepped into the bathroom just as the struggling James had been hoisted aloft by the yelling mob. James saw him and pleaded to him for help. Mr. Long just looked at him expressionless, told Tommy and his crew to lower their voices, and left the bathroom.

When James emerged from the bathroom, covered in excrement and blood, another teacher had escorted him to the principal's office, Mr. Bowling. Although James didn't tell the principal who had done it, he did say that Mr. Long had witnessed it. When Mr. Long was summoned, he denied being there, so no punishment was ever given.

When James and Mr. Long left the room, James to go home and Mr. Long back to his class, James asked him why he didn't stop it or report it, not to mention denying even being there.

"Boys will be boys" he said, "there was no harm done."

James called Wesley and asked him if he would have a driver available for the following day.

"Hey, James my man, glad you called. Kirk wants to do it and I might tag along for the fun of it. What time and where?"

"Twelve a'clock at the Jack in the Box on Woodside Road. The driver parks up on the street behind, probably because the restaurant doesn't like his truck in the parking lot, and he always spends an hour there. That's our time frame. Is there a kid ready at the school?"

"Yeah, what does he need to do?"

"Just to get Mr. Long, the teacher who is on yard duty, to come over to the truck two minutes after we pull up at the fence."

"I could have the boy wait at the fence for us if you like."

"No. I don't want the kid to look suspicious. Kirk or yourself can call him when we're ready, and the kid can just attract Mr. Long's attention to us. That should be enough to get Mr. Long to come over to us."

"Okay, sounds good. Hey man, you're a hero to my pals in East Palo Alto. Remind me sometime never to get on your wrong side. You have friends for life over there. I never thought I'd see the day when that mother fucker cop would get his dues."

"I have no idea what you mean Wesley" replied James, tongue in cheek, "but I would never take you on Wesley, you'd crush me with one hand. Just keep what happened quiet will you?"

"You got it man, but you're owed, and not just by me."

"That reminds me Wesley, check your bank account. It's all safe, so do what you want with it."

"Jeez man, can I be your partner? I don't know what I ever did for you that deserves all these rewards, but thank you James. Just remember that I'm always here for you, you hear me?"

"I hear you Wesley. I'll maybe see you tomorrow then?"

"You want a ride?"

"Sure. Have Kirk pick me up at the same place about 11:45. Okay?

"Okay. Until tomorrow. Thank you James. For everything."

James hung up and going back to his laptop, he anonymously sent the recording of Teco to Youtube for the whole world to see. He also made a call to a different newspaper than the reporter's, to tell them of it. Teco really needed to face the consequences of what he'd done. He then went to check out the storage unit.

The GPS unit was indicating that Jonathon White, or at least his car, was at the storage yard. James set off and had to leave his car parked out of the way, before cautiously walking around the fence with his large hat covering his face. There were many cameras within the storage areas, and some of them probably covered the perimeters. If he was stopped, then he'd be able to say he was taking a short cut alongside the fence to MacDonald's, which was very close by.

Luckily, he spotted the car before his route got too suspicious, and he only stayed long enough to determine what number the unit was. Keeping his hat on, he then went and bought a large coffee before making the same way back to his car. He then drove to Jonathon's work to wait for his return, as he wanted to retrieve the tracking unit.

He was on his way home within seconds after Jonathon had entered through the back door of his store.

James did stop once on his way home, in a very quiet location. He made a call to the police using a prepaid phone, and told them the number and location of the storage unit and what it contained. By this time, it was common knowledge about the disappearance of the trailer, but the surveillance from the distribution center had been somehow tampered with. The police had no leads, so were asking the public to report anyone who was selling the latest video games for a low price. They had nothing. James also told them about the hangar and the trailer.

Jonathon's family seemed to be okay from what James had learned about them, so he resolved to send them an anonymous, but more than generous donation once their husband and father was found guilty.

CHAPTER 20

James did some research for the rest of the afternoon before getting ready to go to Alice's.

He'd been worrying about Alice ever since he'd spoken to her, and was wondering how fragile she would be this evening. James knew it was no easy thing to reveal your past. It was like admitting to being weak and helpless. James had felt for most of his years, that he had a target on his back that he couldn't see but everyone else could, or that there was something dreadfully wrong with him. He thought all kinds of things were to blame. He was ugly. An alien. A leper. Dumb. Too clever. Hideous. A threat. He felt an affinity with the bullied kids who'd finally snapped, then taken a gun to school and started shooting. He despaired when these kids were described as mad, or crazy, because they were different in some way.

No-one wanted to discuss that maybe these kids had a genuine beef. They'd been beaten and bullied to breaking point, in schools that didn't protect them or listen to them. Then everyone is amazed and horrified when they snap and exact their revenge, calling them strange, and weirdo's.

James wasn't elated with some of the things he'd done, but he was feeling freer. It was a relief he felt after dealing with his demons, but now he could see the finishing line. He wasn't haunted any more by a mob of baying tormentors. Now there were just three in his thoughts, and one of those would hopefully be banished the following day.

On the way over to Alice's, James stopped by a wine store and an Indian takeaway. He hoped Alice would like a curry, and that she'd possibly be hungry after the telephone conversation earlier.

He needn't have worried.

Alice loved Indian food and was glad the restaurant had included the naan bread, mango chutney, shaved coconut, and raisins. She was starving and ate more than James did, not even mentioning their earlier phone call. Instead, she talked about her busy afternoon at work. She seemed happier to James somehow, she was more vibrant than normal, and they smiled and laughed all through dinner.

Alice hadn't had time to change before James got there, the only thing she'd done had been to let her hair tumble down. So she was still in her white blouse and maroon skirt when she asked James to take her to bed.

James happily did so, and was even happier when she put on the bedside lamp and told him to undress her.

As he slowly undressed her, she told him that their earlier conversation had been liberating to her, that it felt so good to tell someone about it, who could understand what she went through.

Once he had her down to her frilly laced matching red panties and bra, James undressed himself before continuing with Alice, and she was smiling at him. He thought she would have her eyes closed and be tense, but she was happy, and very relaxed as she watched him take off his clothes.

She stayed very still as he unhooked her bra and slid down her panties, watching his eyes as he took her in, and his gentle hands brushed against her skin.

As he went to kiss her, she shook her head no, told him to wait in a whisper, as she elegantly got onto the bed and lay down on her back, facing him on her elbows. She was still smiling and James couldn't help but admire her new found confidence. Especially so when she raised her knees and parted her legs, telling him she'd been thinking of him all afternoon, and that she needed him to enter her. Now.

It didn't last long, and as James stroked her body as he waited for his body to recover, he asked her if she still had any anger toward Susan Ward. She thought long and hard before replying.

"I do, but not in the same way. I think before I talked to you, that if she'd come into the hospital, or I'd seen her on the street or something, then I may have gone crazy. I don't know, it's hard to say what I would have done, but I've thought for years that I would like to have stabbed her or something. Many times. Now? I don't know. I doubt if I could do her bodily harm, but I would still like her to get her just rewards somehow. What she did to me she has probably done to others, and will continue to do so. I don't like that thought. I don't want her to get away with it, but at the same time I don't want to just kill her. That seems too quick and painless. I would never be able to take her to court either. I don't want the whole world to know what I went through. She would also probably enjoy being tortured, so what's the point of doing that? I do feel better now, but it would be good for her to suffer in some way. I feel relieved now James. It doesn't seem as bad anymore.

Have you got your wind back yet or can I help you along the way?" She asked, changing the subject.

She'd turned onto her side as she asked this and her hand went to his groin, closely followed by her lips and her open mouth.

"Oh, my wind is coming back Alice," he gasped in pleasure, "it's coming back very quickly."

CHAPTER 21

James didn't wake until Alice brought him some coffee as she was about to leave for work. They'd finally made it under the sheets, James felt so good when he woke up, and Alice was radiant.

He saw she was ready for work and tried to persuade her to call in sick, or just arrive late. She had to go but she told him to sleep in a bit longer, or just stay in bed until she got home.

James had plans for the day so he told her he'd pick her up after work the next day, so she would need to pack that evening for the weekend. She was disappointed he wouldn't be there when she got home, but she gave him a lingering, hot wet kiss before she left, and James couldn't wait to see her again.

He didn't doze off after she left, but he did take his time, as he took a shower and made himself some breakfast, cleaning up afterwards in a mannerly fashion.

Once he got home, he found some old clothing that he wanted to throw out and put them on, before he walked down to the pick up location.

Wesley was with Kirk, and he gave James a big bear hug when they arrived, holding him for a couple of minutes and slapping him on the back

"As far as I'm concerned, you're my bro' now James, a close member of my family, and I'll always have your back. Y'hear me?"

"I hear you Wesley, and thank you."

"Hey. It's me giving you thanks. So, are you ready to go?"

"I'm ready, lets get this done."

"So what's the plan?" Wesley asked as they drove away.

"Like I said, we pick up the truck at Jack in the Box, park it at the side of the school yard, your kid tells Mr. Long, and after he comes over to see what we're doing, I have a word with him and then we take the truck back and disappear."

"Sounds good man. I thought I'd bring the car along just in case we get delayed or something. Okay?"

"Sure. Good idea. When you make the call to your kid, tell him to have his phone ready to video record. I want this to go viral."

"I can't wait. Kirk, you make sure you can't be recognized. Do you have a mask James?"

"I brought two. One for Kirk if he needs it."

"I got one dude, but thanks. You got gloves?" asked Kirk.

"Yes," replied James.

They had to wait a few minutes for the truck to show, and as the driver jumped out and made his way around the corner to the restaurant, James casually walked up to the truck and was in it within seconds, having it started as Kirk got to climb in, and he scooted over onto the passenger seat.

After a brief look at the controls, Kirk was driving them away, not taking the quickest route that would have passed the restaurant.

They were pulling up at the school yard within five minutes, followed at a safe distance by Wesley, in the newly stolen car.

When they pulled up, both were already in their ski masks, and as Kirk pressed buttons and pulled levers, James was unhooking the hose and climbing on top of the truck.

Ready, he gave Wesley a thumbs up sign and watched him speak to someone on his cell phone. Mr. Long was approaching within seconds, apparently not in a very good mood.

"What the hell are you doing? You can't park there. Don't you know this is a school?"

Mr. Long, just as James remembered him, still dressed in a shirt, chino's, and blazer.

"Can't hear you man," replied James with his head down, not wanting Mr. Long to see he was in a mask, and the pump wasn't exactly quiet.

Mr. Long came closer to the fence, his face livid with having to deal with these stupid guys and their disgusting septic truck.

"You need to move this thing now" he yelled up toward James.

James revealed his masked face to Mr. Long, and seeing Kirk off to his right, he replied, "Boys will be boys Mr. Long, and men will be men. No harm done. Hit it dude."

Kirk hit the switch as James held on tight to the hose, bracing himself as he felt the contents of the truck surge up the flexible and heavy tube.

As the full contents of that mornings septic tank withdrawal hit him full on the face, Mr. Long fell backwards as James let it all go. The smell was atrocious and he almost gagged, but he kept the hose pointed at Mr. Long, covering him in several weeks worth of piss and shit.

James was so focused on his job, it wasn't until he was back in the truck driving away that he realized what had just happened.

Kirk was whooping and hollering, laughing and beating the steering wheel.

"Man, that was the coolest fuckin thing I ever seen man" he yelled in James's direction.

"He had it coming" replied James, beginning to smile at the memory.

"Man, I thought I'd been in deep shit before, but I ain't ever been in that much shit" laughed Kirk.

James laughed with him, and they were still laughing when they parked the truck. The driver would have some explaining to do, but he would have an alibi so they weren't worried about him.

Jumping into the car, Wesley was also laughing, as he commented, "You guys stink."

"Not as much as that fuckin teach" laughed Kirk.

"Did you get it recorded Wesley?" Asked James.

"Me and half the school. Where the fuck did you come up with that idea?" Giggled Wesley. "That was the funniest god damn thing I ever seen."

"Cool, huh?" Laughed the relieved James.

"Coolest thing ever. I don't know what that guy did to you James, but I will never, ever, fuck you up" Wesley added, smiling and laughing still at the guy swimming in a whole lot of shit.

CHAPTER 22

James was very unsure what to do about Susan Ward. From what he'd found out about her, and Alice's painful memories, it was clear that she was no ordinary woman. James thought he needed to get inside her mind somehow to hurt her from the inside out. It would be no easy task, and he didn't think he'd be able to accomplish it alone. He didn't like enlisting help, unless he was certain he could trust them as much as Wesley.

Unfortunately, Wesley would be no help with the scheme that was running through his head. James could easily ruin Susan Ward financially, but that wouldn't be enough, there had to be something else.

He would make maybe a couple of phone calls to see if he could find someone suitable for the idea running through his head, and if no-one was interested, or didn't have the nerve, then he'd think of something else.

Apart from working on that, he threw some clothing away, some of it smelly, and cleaned his apartment. Then he packed a small suitcase before picking up Alice for the weekend.

Although Alice had her case packed, she wanted to change before leaving, so James picked her up at her home shortly after she finished work.

Like James, she wore blue jeans. Whereas his were comfort fitting, hers were tight and emphasized her slim figure. She teamed it with a plain white top, toeless heeled sandals, and carried a white cable knit sweater over her arm as she emerged from her building to get into the car. James got out to greet her with a kiss and a hug, taking her case, and depositing it with his own in the trunk. James wore a blue tee shirt with the Apple insignia over his jeans, and he had a leather jacket ready in the trunk for the cool of Half Moon Bay, which was just down the coast from San Francisco.

Alice, to James's eye looked gorgeous, and he wasted no time in telling her so. She blushed slightly on hearing his compliment but smiled broadly as well, she'd spent a great deal of time to appear natural.

James stopped fairly quickly after picking up Alice, at the Village Pub in Woodside to have dinner, before continuing on to Half Moon Bay.

The pub has a very good reputation for it's food in the San Francisco Area, but it is also close to where James grew up, although he had never dined in there before.

As they were early, they managed to get a table very easily, and they shared an Alaskan Halibut, which was superbly cooked and presented.

Alice had a couple of glasses of Chardonnay with her dinner, James just had water.

James, being in his home village, talked about his childhood during their meal, but mainly the pleasant memories of the animals and his mom when she wasn't working.

When they left, he took Alice by his old home, and although they could only see it from a distance, the new owners looked like they were taking care of the place, as it had been freshly painted and looked in great shape.

It didn't take long from there to get to Half Moon Bay, and it's a very pleasant route through the small mountains, woods, and many working farms.

James had entered the hotel's address on his GPS, and it looked as good as it did on the website when they arrived, and they put on their warm outer layers to ward off the chill.

The hotel was the Landis Shores Oceanfront Inn on the North Coast of the Bay, and it was lovely.

James had ordered the pampering package, so when they entered their room Alice was very delighted to find the king sized bed covered with red rose petals, champagne on ice, candles, chocolates, and delightful bath products.

The room itself was on a corner of the second floor. It had a balcony facing the pacific ocean, a fireplace with the gas fire already lit, and a large bathroom with a huge tub and separate shower. James also mentioned to Alice, with a devious smile, that the walls were soundproof.

As James opened the champagne bottle and poured their glasses, Alice kicked off her shoes and removed her sweater, before sprawling out on the huge bed, in total glee.

She got up as James approached with the glasses, taking one as he raised his glass and said, "To a glorious weekend!"

They clinked their glasses and took a sip, before James gave her a long kiss. After they took another drink, he put both their glasses down, and undressed her where she stood, taking his time with each item of clothing. She watched him closely as he slowly disrobed her, seeing his delight as he explored her with his eyes, hands, lips, and tongue. She had never let another man do this to her, at least not as intimately as James was now doing, so it was a new experience and she relished it.

Once James too was naked, they rolled around on the large bed getting covered in petals which stuck to their sweaty skin. James followed Alice's orgasm shortly after hers, and after lying entwined for a few minutes, they got off the bed and put on the robes that were provided. James filled their glasses, and they took their drinks and the chocolates out to the balcony, and watched the sun disappear for the night.

They didn't stay out there for too long, it got very chilly, so they settled in front of the fire and James ordered another bottle of champagne from the front desk, as they held hands and watched the flames.

Later, Alice ran the bath, lit some candles, and climbed into it with James very close behind, adding more hot water when it started to feel cool. They made love again while still in the bath, then washed each other before retiring naked to their bed for some much needed sleep.

The following day, after more love making and a scrumptious breakfast in the Inn, James took Alice horse riding on the beach. Neither had ever ridden before so the instructor joined them, but they had never ached so much on dismounting, although they had thoroughly enjoyed the experience.

They hadn't needed lunch after their huge breakfasts, but they did have dinner at the Costanera, which was a highly regarded Peruvian restaurant on the Bay, and it was delicious.

On returning to their room, James purchased a bottle of Cabernet from the Inn, and they watched a DVD together before making love yet again before falling asleep.

It was with a great deal of reluctance on both parts when the following morning they had to check out of the Inn, stopping at the Miramar Beach Restaurant for a late lunch, before heading home.

"This has been a wonderful weekend James," Alice commented as she ate her Bootleggers Shrimp Sandwich, "can we do this again sometime?"

"I'd like to think of this as the first of many weekends Alice, this has been so much fun."

James was also eating a sandwich, a crab melt that kept dripping down the side of his mouth.

"Can I ask you a favor James?" She asked softly.

"Sure. What do you need?"

"Would you come over to my parents house next Sunday? They went to England once, and when they came back they started doing this late Sunday lunch of various roasts. One week it might be pork, another beef, then chicken, and so on. They've done it ever since they came back, and it's become a tradition. I'd love for you to meet them and to come and join us."

"Shouldn't you be there today?"

"No. I don't go every week, but they always ask me over. Will you come with me?" She pleaded.

"Of course I will. You sure they won't mind?"

"They'll be thrilled to bits. Thank you James, it means a lot to me."

"Then it's a date. Just don't ask me to ride a horse for a while, I'm still aching from doing that," he grimaced.

"So am I," she whispered, looking around to make sure no one was in earshot, "but I thought it was from way too much sex."

"That's a good ache" James whispered back. "You turn me on so much, I might even be up to more of that when I get you home" he smiled.

"Then let's go lover boy, there's not much of the day left," she winked.

CHAPTER 23

James didn't get to his home until the following day, after Alice had dragged herself off to work. He couldn't remember if he had ever felt as happy as he felt now, even with a couple of things still gnawing away at his mind.

Although he fully realized that some of his actions had been extreme to say the least, he felt justified, and had no remorse. He'd been pushed and pushed to his breaking point, and had gotten his revenge with those who weren't sorry for what they'd done to him, and probably to numerous others. James had been able to do this to his tormentors, but he was well aware that other victims would never be able to get their revenge.

Lately, he'd been reading on websites about other victims of bullies, whose only crime was being different to almost everyone else. Thinner, fatter, taller, smaller, good looking, not attractive, slower, faster, poorer, cleverer, there was always some kind of inane reason.

The families or the victims themselves were beginning to raise their voices, but there still wasn't much being done about it. All the authorities were voicing the right thing, saying it was intolerable and they wouldn't stand for it, but in reality, the problem was growing despite their words.

It was bad enough for the able bodied, but James read about autistic kids, handicapped children, the deaf, the blind, the sick, who also had to cope somehow with bullies. He couldn't imagine how difficult it was for them.

James's opinion was that most, if not all the blame, was with the bullies parents. Children copy the behavior of their mothers and fathers, and if they see or hear them talking down to others, then it's natural to follow their lead. If parents don't show respect to certain people, their kids will generally be the same.

It used to be that if children didn't get the right parenting, then the schools would teach them the correct way. It was a part of being a teacher. If kids went to school with this preconceived idea that different colors or religions were wrong, then they were educated in what was right, and no one disputed the authority of the teacher.

James couldn't remember those days. When he attended school there wasn't much respect given to the teachers. Everyone wore what they wanted to, or could afford, there was no real punishment, and no kid was ever afraid of any teacher. It was other kids they were afraid of.

To James, it seemed like too much power had been given to the children and to the parents, which to him was all wrong. Everyone got prizes, there were no winners or losers, and there were no reprimands or criticisms. If there were, the over protective parents would be knocking on the principal's door.

In some respect, James could understand why Mr. Long had chosen to look the other way. To lie to the Principal about it was another matter. As for the Principal himself, James knew he wouldn't have done anything, because he never did. School nowadays was all politics, and unless you had a large and powerful lobby, you were never heard, or were just ignored. Who gives a damn about the minority child with drugged up parents, when the bully is the school quarterback taking them to the championships, and bringing in money? It was all politics and if there was anything James disliked, apart from bankers, it was a politician.

Politicians pretend to know what it's like to have no money, or no health insurance, or to lose a home to a corrupt bank.

They have no idea. With free healthcare, free prescriptions, legal insider trading, pensions for life that match their salaries, backers throwing money at them to protect their industries, all expenses paid into six figures, they can't possibly comprehend how hard life is for people. They just pretend to, purely for the votes.

With what he was reading, James was increasingly appalled. Everywhere he looked, it seemed like everyone was bullying someone. All the billions of dollars being accrued by those at the top, were at the expense of those at the bottom. It was all profit margin, pure and simple greed.

James couldn't pinpoint when this attitude of "I'm all right, so screw everyone else" attitude started. It wasn't everyone by any means, but it was by enough to keep the status quo getting worse. If these people were ever asked, they would tell everyone to get a job and pay for their services like they did, that they weren't owed anything by anyone. All very true, but it's not that easy to find a job paying a decent salary, or to even pay enough for your rent, never mind any health insurance. Nor is it easy to pick yourself up from losing your home because your boss wanted to make more profits, so your job was outsourced.

Because some people have it easy, they think it's the same for everyone else.

James read several postings from all around the US. It was a tip of the iceberg with what people were saying, in all kinds of circumstances. It ranged from many people denied any further unemployment payments, even though they still couldn't find anyone to hire them, to others who owed thousands of dollars because of illness. James read that over 50% of bankruptcies are caused by health care costs.

One story about bullying in particular, hit home to James, partly because it was about a child who was suffering.

The child in question lived in Florida and his parents didn't know where to turn to. It seemed that one of their children was an autistic boy who the authorities thought, and insisted, should go to a regular school. The boy had been happy to go to regular school because he quite rightly thought that he was no different to anybody else, except that he was a little slow, and sometimes said the wrong things. He didn't look any different to anyone else, he was just autistic.

So he was being bullied. Not just by one person. There were several, and he was being beaten up on a regular basis. He didn't think his parents should worry or complain, he could handle it, and he didn't mind being hurt. His siblings who attended the same school tried to protect him, but as they weren't in the same class or grade, it was difficult for them. So he was beaten, repeatedly.

His parents reported to, and complained about his treatment to the Principal, and anyone else they could find. They would tell them who had done the beatings, and show them the pictures of their young boy with his cuts and bruises. Nothing was ever done. Nobody suspended. Nobody expelled. The last time, three days ago, the boy was beaten unconscious and still the school would do nothing. The only thing that they said, was that the boy had instigated the beatings by saying something inappropriate. Like it was his own fault for being autistic.

The parents had no idea what to do next. They were being denied requests to change schools, they couldn't afford to have him privately educated, or to move, and they didn't have the knowledge or the time to home school him.

The poor kid could take care of himself one on one, but not against a group. His teachers knew he was autistic, but obviously didn't know what that meant, nor did they teach the other children about it.

James looked at the advice the parents were getting, and they were mostly being told to hang in there and to keep complaining. To go to the media, whatever it took to be heard. One asshole commented that it was their fault the kid was autistic and it was God punishing them for their ways, as his kids were perfect.

James replied to the parents using a new email address, and asked if they'd thought about naming and shaming the perpetrators.

When he received an email back shortly after, asking what he meant, he replied again.

"Dear frantic parents,

As I was bullied all of my childhood and into my adult years, I have a deep empathy for your son. When schools don't listen, or are too afraid to do anything about it, then it leaves you with little you can do. As others have mentioned, you could take him out of school, or even try to sue the school. However, that would cost you money and time with no guarantee of winning.

You could also move to a different school district, but then you could also find yourself in the same situation and why should you have to move? If like you mentioned, you don't have the money to move, then your options are further limited.

What I meant by naming and shaming is by doing a public naming of the bullies, providing you have witnesses who will back you up, and posting the bullies names and pictures on the streets, or in the social media. Doing the social media would be easier. Everybody tweets and does Facebook these days, so humiliate them and their parents. Use your smart phones to record what happens on video, and post them on YouTube. If the parents of the bullies threaten you with court, let them. You would have the witnesses and the video evidence, so the onus would be on them to prove their child didn't do it. Very difficult to do. Then if they stupidly did and lost, you'd have lawyers chasing after you to sue them for damages.

Some of these parents will have a certain social standing. They won't want to be known as the parents of someone who beats up an autistic child. The school will also be humiliated for not having done anything to stop it, and maybe other parents will demand they do so, and involve the media.

Tell me what you think.
David."

It wasn't until the following day when he checked the inbox for that email address, but after reading the reply a couple of times he set to work.

CHAPTER 24

Susan Ward was happy with her life. In her eyes it was practically perfect.

She was still very beautiful, and even after having two children her body was envied by most other women who had never been able to regain their pre-child shape. Susan had of course undergone a grueling training routine to do it, but there were no signs of her being a mother. No stretch marks, no visible scars, no sagging breasts or bottom.

She had received some help from a very skilled surgeon, but she was very proud of her slim figure and size two clothing. She looked not dissimilar to Victoria Beckham, just a little taller and bigger. She'd kept her hair long though, hadn't gone to a bob cut or anything, so when she had it down it stayed close to her head.

During the day, Susan mostly kept her hair in a bun or clipped to the top of her head. In the evenings, she would let it down, or do a ponytail, depending on her mood.

Although she was slender, she was way stronger than she looked. Her long manicured fingers belied the fact that she had a grip like a vice, and she could run for miles, which she did and very often.

Susan was a very good actress although she never set foot in a theater unless she went to a show. During the day, with her hair up, wearing very light make up and business suits, she was to all practical purposes, one of the thousands of other executive women in New York. On certain nights, once she'd stepped out of her family home, the make up would be changed. To dark smoky eyes, with long black eyelashes shielding her blue eyes, and vivid lipstick. Her clothing too would change. From looking very approachable, she went to dangerous and scary, which was exactly the look she wanted.

After leaving college, Susan had hightailed it to New York City where she felt destined for and belonged. She had been accepted into an advertising agency before even leaving college, and after perusing the ads in the newspapers, she found someone very much like herself who needed a room mate. It proved to be beneficial to them both.

Susan worked her way up the ladder in the advertising company, in a very short time. Some thought it highly suspicious, and it was, but it was there she met her husband. She didn't really like the job or the agency, so once she was married, she set up her own job as a party planner, got an office, and went to work.

Susan still preferred women to men. Her husband wasn't aware of that at all and she liked being married. She certainly loved her little children Joshua and Mattie, who were just eight and six years old, and she liked their social standing. Her husband Eli, was now a partner at the agency and making a great deal of money. Most of the clients were as Jewish as he and the other partners were, and they lived in the lower east side of Manhattan, which was also mainly Jewish.

Susan had taken up the Jewish faith, she'd had to really, but although she regularly attended with her family, she wasn't at all religious.

Her room mate when she first arrived in New York, was called Tuesday. She said her parents gave her that name because that was the day she was conceived on. Tuesday thought it was stupid, but she'd gotten used to the name, and it didn't sound as bad as when she was younger.

Tuesday was older than Susan but was still an attractive and head turning blonde. She'd never had children or been married, but she'd needed a room mate because her younger brother had drug problems, and she was paying for the rehabilitation as their parents couldn't afford it. Tuesday was in shape, a size larger than Susan, well formed. She also had blue eyes and sharp features, but was not prone to smiling very often.

Tuesday worked in an S & M club.

Although she played both roles, Tuesday much preferred being the masochist, which was music to Susan's ears. What Susan had done through school to other girls, as the sadist, Tuesday was getting well paid for it. Not to mention getting the pleasure and it being legal. Tuesday introduced Susan to the owners of where she worked, and to the other girls. She also took her shopping for the Lycra and leather outfits, and very soon, Susan was working two jobs and finding the one in the advertising agency to be very boring indeed.

When Susan and Tuesday weren't working, Susan would go home and would have Tuesday obey her commands, which they both thoroughly enjoyed. Tuesday too preferred women to men, and she was more than happy to oblige Susan and take some pleasurable pain.

Tuesday knew about Susan's ambitions, and although she wasn't happy when Susan got married and moved out, she also knew it wasn't because of love or herself. By that time, Tuesday had paid the rehab fee, her brother was keeping clean, and she had money in the bank. She also continued to see Susan, publicly and privately.

With the money she'd earned from her two jobs, Susan secretly bought her own club, and called it the Dungeon of Total Fear. The party planning company was for her customers who wanted an in-home experience, which was very lucrative, but not very legal. Most of the parties were wild, drugs would often be used, and discretion was of the utmost importance. Susan knew that some of the people she hired for the club would never be suitable for the parties, so she never asked them. It would have been too risky. They had to like what they were doing, and Susan would often see that some of them didn't. It was just an extra buck for them. That was okay in the club, but not at the parties.

Having the party planning business was a great excuse for Susan. You can't plan a party and not supervise it. Her husband Eli didn't understand why Susan couldn't just stay home and look after the children, as he earned plenty. Susan said she needed to work, and as they had a great nanny for the children then why not. She also did parties for their friends which were totally innocent, but made her very popular in the community.

Susan loved being a dominatrix, and when she could, she really liked to hurt her clients. Some didn't like to be hurt too much, others did, and although she had many men clients, she much preferred the women.

Some days she could barely wait to get to the club if it was a favorite client waiting. She also liked the parties and the craziness of it all.

Many of the clients were very well to do and had connections. Apart from celebrities, there were lawyers, priests, cops, top executives, politicians and others. Her club was left alone, and no one came sniffing around with questions.

This particular night a new girl was starting who also worked at a high end escort agency. Tuesday was now working for Susan as her assistant, and had said what a striking woman she was, and that she'd be a perfect addition. Susan, on hearing about her short, spiky red hair, was intrigued. She'd always had a thing for redheads, so was looking forward to meeting her.

As the owner, Susan had her own dressing room at the club, the others shared a room that was well equipped with closets, make up tables, showers, and full length mirrors.

Although her client wouldn't arrive for another hour or so, Susan got ready early.

Susan had many costumes, but the one she put on tonight was one of her favorites, for one of her best clients.

It was a high necked Lycra costume in black, the sides were cut out, and she could tear off parts of the Lycra to reveal her breasts, with another panel between her legs to reveal her shaved crutch. She teamed it with self holding, thigh high fishnet stockings, and knee high boots with stiletto heels. The costume was sleeveless, so she added some studded bracelets, and wore a mask that only exposed her eyes, nostrils, and mouth. She had her hair up, so looked very stern. Inside, she felt as sexy as hell.

The club itself was large, and it was set in a basement under two stores. Susan had tried to make it look as much like a dungeon as possible, with stone walls and real looking cell doors with bars to peek through. Each cell held different apparatus, and they were quite spacious.

All the walls in the club were covered in objects of torture, like thumb screws, studded clubs, whips, and clamps. There were pictures of people in agony on racks, fingernails being pulled by pliers, and folks chained to the wall. Everything imaginable was on display and meant to scare.

The entrance lounge was quite different. It felt warm and cozy, with comfortable chairs, and tables with shaded lamps. There was carpet on the floor and a licensed bar, with large bathrooms for the clients to change in or to refresh. Everybody was checked in on arriving, and their coats taken if need be, which was generally the case as most showed up in their outfits, but hidden under a raincoat.

They could accommodate walk-ins and Susan had extra staff for that, but they couldn't take very many, and usually asked them to come another night after taking credit card details and I.D. for their age.

Once the clients had arrived and checked in, whoever was taking care of them would be summoned, and they would come to the lounge to meet them and take them to their cell. If they wanted to take a peek at someone who was screaming or yelling or whatever, they were allowed to. It was all open to view.

Susan met Tuesday close to her own personal cell, which unlike the others was partially private. It was the only cell you couldn't see into if Susan didn't want you to, but you could hear what was happening through the vents. All the walls and ceilings were soundproof, the lighting was on the dim side, but it was all well ventilated and temperature controlled, with sprinklers and emergency exits.

Susan was tonight in a maroon costume that barely concealed anything. It was a full costume, but her bottom was fully visible as were most of her breasts. Even with her mask on, Susan knew her instantly, but the woman she was with she didn't know, but really wanted to.

Tuesday introduced her as Candy, which was a fake name, as most of the girls, and guys, try to protect themselves. Susan herself would only be called Milady by her clients.

Even though she was in a full black leather outfit and a partial mask, Susan could tell that Candy not only had a great figure, but she was also a looker as well. Although her eyes too were darkened by make up, her green eyes were warm and inviting, her nose was pert and cute, and her lips were full and enticing. Her hair wasn't long, it was as spiky as Tuesday had said it was, but she was tall and only showed a little skin. Susan wanted to see more of her.

After a brief introduction, Tuesday said her client had arrived and that she was going to take Candy with her. The client in question would love someone else there, so it would be good for Candy to see what was required of her, and if it would be suitable for her.

Susan concurred with this, told Candy to just go and enjoy herself, and she'd check up with them later.

No one at the club knew it, not even Tuesday, but Susan had tiny cameras installed in the cells purely for safety. Quite a number of the clients were elderly, or out of shape, and if they had a heart attack or something, then Susan needed to know that one of her staff hadn't induced it. Then there was also drugs and money to consider. All her staff got good money and weren't being cheated, so she didn't want them dealing drugs, or asking for more money from the clients. There were no extras in the club, Susan could lose her license for that, so she had to keep checking. She didn't though, keep the recordings for very long, and she didn't need to blackmail anyone.

Susan watched from her dressing room laptop as Tuesday led the client into the room, followed by Candy.

The client was female, tiny, and she was wearing a Lycra costume that had a big V opening from the neck to just above her vagina. Her legs were thin, she had a covering over her eyes, and she wore big heels to give her more height. The costume was also backless.

As the cell door closed, Tuesday changed her demeanor. Susan couldn't hear anything, but Tuesday immediately grabbed the client's hair from behind, pulling her head back and down. Tuesday seemed to say something to Candy, who stepped forward and fondled the client as Tuesday continued to grip the woman's mousy hair.

Susan watched Candy. She seemed to enjoy what she was doing and she teased the woman with her lips. The client obviously wanted to touch, but Candy and Tuesday wouldn't let her.

Tuesday and Candy swapped positions and Tuesday also fondled the client, slowly, her hands sliding under the Lycra.

Susan looked at the time, her client would be here shortly, if not already, and she looked at the phone on the table that would shortly ring.

Tuesday was now peeling off the client's costume as Candy pulled her head back with her hair again. The client was grimacing which was good.

The client was small breasted with rings on her nipples, that Tuesday and Candy pulled on with their spare hands. Once she was naked, Tuesday grabbed one of her wrists and put it into the cushioned wrist brace above her head, quickly followed by her other hand, so that the client was now standing with her arms above her head. Tuesday nodded to Candy, and they both took a leg each, raising them so that the client was now hanging face down as they clamped her ankles into more braces. Tuesday went to the wall and lowered the clamp apparatus to about hip height. The braces were on ropes so they could swing the client around if need be, but Tuesday grabbed her by the hair again and made her lick her breasts, pulling them out from her costume to expose the nipples.

As she did this, Candy came into the picture with a dildo from behind the client and between her outstretched legs.

Susan's phone rang.

Cursing to herself, she closed the laptop and went to greet her client. It was a man tonight, a man of god, and he liked pain. Not for him the brushes and paddles that would hurt, but not too much. He liked, and felt he deserved, the whip that Susan wielded that cut and left welts. He also liked the cattle prodder that she would use to shock his genitals. She was the dominatrix and he was the servant. She was the best and she'd get him screaming in pain and remorse. He loved this club.

CHAPTER 25

James felt he had another new purpose to life with something very close to his heart. The boy and his parents in Florida had really hit home and he so wanted to do something for them.

The parents came up trumps. They found some witnesses, and one of them had also gotten one of the beatings on their cellphone. The witness just wanted to stay anonymous. The victim was brave, possibly foolhardy, in trying to stand up to the four kids who were punching and kicking him. The leader had first called to the kid by calling him a retard, and when the boy just carried on walking, the leader and his pals rushed him from behind.

James had been in that position many times, but he'd ran at the first shot or chance. This boy had tried to stand his ground against all the odds, and had paid for it. How on earth the school could ignore this was incomprehensible, but it was redneck country, so who knew.

The parents had a computer and knew about the social media, but hadn't used it much to their advantage. James told them what they needed to do, and helped them to set it up with a dedicated Facebook page, a twitter campaign, YouTube, and a bombardment of the press. The boy's younger sister also set up her own "Stop Bullying" page.

James created a website for bullied victims, with advice and links to help them, encouraging everyone to tell their story, and to name names if they had the evidence.

He also was able to find the parents of the Florida bullies and their Facebook addresses, along with the principal of the school. He sent them all the link to the YouTube feed, and warned them that there was now a nationwide campaign to rid all schools of bullies, and they were being targeted.

It was all very exciting for James, he was keeping himself anonymous, but he was only too happy to help, and the website began to attract visitors.

Alice thought it was all a great idea and volunteered to help in any way she could. James had her write a page for the website, telling the parents what to watch for with their children, physically and mentally, and what to do if they displayed any of the symptoms of being bullied. Such as being withdrawn, closing their computer screen abruptly, or no friends. If they were already being bullied, then it was imperative that they sought help in any shape or form, but to support their child in the right way.

The sight though wasn't just for bullied children, it was also for adults. The kids who bully in school go on to bully at work, making life miserable for millions of adults. Hating to go to work could be put down to many reasons, but when unreasonable demands are made of you, or you're made to feel guilty about taking vacation time, or you're continuously belittled or criticized, all are signs of being bullied. You can literally go from cradle to grave being the victim of someone.

It was never going to stop until the parents stopped it and started to set an example, or there was more intervention by those who witness it. James thought that if maybe he could show people where they were going wrong, that it's not right to mistreat people, then he would be happy in some measure.

The parents in Florida later informed James that the local press were now asking questions and putting pressure on the school. The principal was trying to deny that he knew anything, but the evidence was there for all to see, and he was beginning to look stupid with his answers.

Other parents were now contacting the boy's parents, saying how sorry they were, and other kids were coming forward with their own stories.

The whole city become involved, it was the main talking point, but more tellingly, the boy hadn't been beaten up lately or been called any names. Something was finally being done.

James was still fixed on doing something about Susan Ward, he couldn't let her go, he was even beginning to think he could feel the welts on Alice's back which had long since disappeared, physically, if not mentally.

James's friend, the escort, who he only knew as Crystal, had informed him that her friend in New York, Candy, was now working for Susan in her club.

When James had asked Crystal if she knew or could recommend anyone in New York, it was more out of hope than anything else. He'd had a different plan to go to, but this would be better, and when Crystal said it would be perfect for her friend James went ahead with it. That James would have to pay a sizable sum for their services was of no consequence to him. He had money and this would be well spent.

He didn't want Candy to do anything dangerous, although working in a S & M club created its own dangers. Candy was into that though, which was why she was perfect. James just wanted to know what went on, an angle he could use, so any information, however small, was valuable to him.

Candy had already reported to Crystal that the club was working above board, but she'd been welcomed into the club and was slowly getting to know everyone. She had heard from a couple of the employees that the private parties were the most lucrative, but the owner of the club, Susan, would only take the most trusted to them as the parties got very chaotic and nobody could tell tales. As these parties usually occurred on nights when the club was open, not everybody could go, no phones or cameras were allowed, and the address was never disclosed. Whoever went, was taken in a darkened out limo from the club.

Candy also mentioned to Crystal that although Susan had her own dressing room cum office in the club, she did her business from elsewhere, but she didn't know where it was. Somebody had mentioned she ran a party planning business, but they didn't know what it was called.

It was more information than James had hoped for and he began searching through the party planners in New York. It was a lengthy list, but he enjoyed researching and knew he would find her. He also realized he would have to go to New York and do something illegal again. He needed to know as much as possible about Susan Ward before traversing the country.

CHAPTER 26

James was nervous about meeting Alice's family, it was totally new to him to be doing that sort of thing. Alice herself hadn't seemed nervous at all to his mind, she just looked forward to taking him over.

Although James spent the night with Alice, he went home to change before they went, and he looked at himself long and hard in the mirror before Alice picked him up. She thought he might like to have a drink or two before and during lunch, to calm him down.

Alice was happy that James was nervous about meeting her family. It proved to her that he cared, that he wanted to impress, and it also helped her to keep her nerves at bay. This was a first for her as well. She'd never liked anyone enough to take home with her, and she knew her mom was fussing about and driving everyone crazy.

Alice had told James not to dress up, but he still looked smart in his stone dockers and open necked dress shirt, and she told him how handsome he looked when he stepped into her car. Alice herself was in blue jeans and a black top.

Her parents house wasn't far away from where James was living, and it only took ten minutes before she was parking by the sidewalk. The journey had been very quiet.

The house itself was very modest. It was just one story, an old ranch style home, with a well tended grass lawn on either side of the walkway to the front door. There was no fence and no porch, but there was a screen door. A double garage had two trucks parked outside, and as they exited the car, Alice pointed out that her brother's truck was the higher of the two.

They held hands as they walked up to the house, the front door opened, and the woman who was greeting them called out "They're here!"

James was carrying two bottles of wine and some chocolates in a bag, and wished one of the bottles was open so that he could take a swig as he got closer. Alice took her hand away to open the screen door and hug her mom, before turning back around to introduce him. James stepped inside.

Alice's mom was shorter than she, but apart from her hair, looked like her daughter, just older. Her hair was dark brown and starting to grey, but she'd kept her figure well, and had a welcoming smile. Along with a warm hug.

"So happy to meet you James. Call me Tina and welcome. Come on inside and make yourself at home," she greeted him.

"Nice to meet you too Tina, I have something for you," James replied, handing over the bag of wine and chocolates.

"Oh you shouldn't have, there was no need, but thank you James, that's very kind of you and I love these chocolates. Now come on, you need to meet everyone."

Alice led the way, but it was a small house, so almost immediately they were in the family living room that just had a counter between it and the kitchen. James could smell the lunch cooking and felt hungry, as Alice's father got up from the armchair.

"James, this is my dad, and that thing on the sofa is my little brother John," Alice smiled.

Her brother was lying flat out on the couch and he stayed there as Alice's father came forward with his hand outstretched. He was the reason that Alice and her brother had red hair. His was short now and rapidly receding, he was tall, but had a middle aged spread. Like Tina, he had a warm smile.

"Call me Bill, James, no formality around here, and glad to meet you." He shook James's hand. "It's good to put a face to someone I've been hearing about for the last couple of weeks. John, get your lazy ass off the couch and come and say hello."

James suspected that Alice's mother and father were slightly overdressed than they normally were. Tina was wearing a skirt and blouse, and Bill wore a polo shirt over his slacks. Her little brother though, was probably as he normally was. He wasn't little though. He was as tall, if not taller than his father, and was well filled out. His red hair was a long straggly mess, his jeans were barely holding on to his hips, and his tee shirt was adorned with a group's name that James had never heard of.

"Hey dude," he greeted James, shaking his hand, "I hear you're warming up my frigid sister."

James laughed as John was admonished by everyone else, before retreating to the couch to resume watching the football that was on the television.

Bill went to open the patio door to the small garden that was visible, after hearing a frantic scratching. A little dog burst into the room, crying and excited all at the same time.

James crouched down to meet him, a mixed beagle in tan, black, and white.

"He doesn't bite or lick, he just sniffs. His name is Niner," explained Bill.

Niner gave James a quick sniff before heading to his main target, Alice, fussing around her and making his peculiar crying noises.

James watched as Alice played with her friend, a smile on his face.

"Why is he called Niner?" He asked, to no one in particular.

"For the 49ers" replied John, who was trying to attract the dog's attention by beating the sofa with a hand, "it was my idea and everyone thought it suited him."

Bill offered James a drink, which he accepted, a cold beer from the fridge.

Alice, after calming down the dog, praised her mom for the table setting by the side of the kitchen, the flowers she'd done as a centerpiece, and was flabbergasted when her mom got some appetizers out of the fridge and offered them around.

It was only a clam dip and a spinach dip, but she'd never done this before a lunch, so it caught everyone out, John telling James he should come over more often if this was going to happen.

James felt at ease. They were just a normal family trying to get by, and James could understand why Alice felt so proud of them, and grateful for enabling her to go to college.

He sat down with the two males as Alice helped her mother, and watched some of the football. He may have never played, but he enjoyed the game and knew the rules and the players, so was able to make comments about what was happening.

When Tina told everyone to go and sit down as lunch was ready, James opened a bottle of the wine he'd brought, and poured a glass for Alice, her mother and himself. John was delighted when James offered him some, declining, but telling his parents that at least someone in the house realized he was an adult. Bill said he would stick to his beer.

Tina had plated everyone a garden salad and told James to help himself to one of the bottles of salad dressing that was on the table. James and Alice were sitting together on one side of the rectangular table, her brother opposite, and her parents at either end. It wasn't a long table, the size of the house dictated that, so everyone was in close contact.

Once Tina finished her salad she got up, and asked her husband to carve the meat in the kitchen. He got up to do so, and Alice collected all the plates, putting them straight into the dishwasher.

As Bill removed the silver foil that had been covering the beef, Tina put some vegetables into dishes. Alice put them on the table with some large spoons to retrieve the contents, and Bill asked James how he liked his beef.

Very quickly, everyone's place had half a plate of steaming roast beef on it. Tina told James to help himself to the vegetables, which he did, and passed the dishes in turn to John, as the others slowly joined them. Alice sat down with a steaming jug of gravy, and Tina sat last with a plate of what looked like small hot pastries of some sort.

Niner the dog took his place at Tina's side, waiting hopefully for tidbits to be handed down to him.

"We went to England once," she explained as she handed James the plate, "and we were invited to a Sunday lunch with some friends we met there. We had a meal just like this, and they explained that these things were called Yorkshire Puddings. They are really similar to a pancake mix, but roasted in muffin tins. Seems they started to do them in England when meat was rationed, so to fill up the men, they made these alongside the meager amounts of beef. They are very filling and they soak up the gravy. They only do them with beef, which is a shame, but I have heard that Nordstrom's make them, and offer them with jelly."

"Yes, they do, but they call them popovers, and they look like these," replied James, "but they are way bigger and they serve them cold with strawberry jelly."

"I told James you did a roast meal every Sunday, mom," interjected Alice, "and that it varies from chicken to pork."

"I think it's a great idea Tina, and compliments to you on this meal. It's delicious" James said, after swallowing a mouthful. "These puddings are great with the gravy."

"Thank you James," Tina beamed, "you'll have to come again."

"I'd love to" he added.

"Hey sis" said John, "did you see what happened to that dick Long from school?"

"Language John, we have company" he was told by his mother.

"No. What happened to him?" Asked Alice.

"I'll show you on my phone, it's so cool." John handed over his phone.

"I think your sister can watch it later" Tina told him.

"Then tell me John, the video can wait." Alice put the phone down on the table.

"Some truck came to the school fence during lunch break, so Long goes over to throw his weight around and tell them to get lost. Next thing you know, they're spraying all this crap at him until he's covered in it. Practically the whole school was there watching."

"What do you mean by crap? Was it a garbage truck?" Asked the intent Alice.

"No. It was crap. One of them machines that empties shit from houses. It stunk to high heaven."

"You mean a septic tank emptier? Oh my god, they emptied a septic tank over him?"

"They sure did. I thought he was going to drown in it."

"Did you hear about this James? Have you seen it?" Alice asked.

"No. I don't always keep up with the local news. Can I see the video later John, please?"

Before John could answer, Bill gave further news.

"That wasn't the end of it. When the police arrived and no one could, or wouldn't, tell them who did it, they demanded to be shown the security tapes, and found stuff on the computer of the principal that got him fired, and Long suspended. I don't know whether it's true, but I heard on the grapevine that the principal had some porn on his computer, but he also had some tape of Long having sex with someone in his classroom. Everyone thinks it's a schoolgirl, but he's suspended until they find out. He's probably out on his ear even if it's an adult. Can you pass me the gravy please James."

James passed it to him and helped himself to some more roasted potatoes and carrots.

"That doesn't surprise me at all," came in Alice, "he was always flirting, and the principal was useless."

"We know that Alice," added her mom, "he would never listen to us. So who's for seconds? Would you like some more beef James? There's plenty left."

"I have no room left Tina, but this has been great. By the time I've finished what's on my plate, I'll have had plenty. It is really delicious, thank you."

"I'll have some more" John chipped in.

"You can help yourself, and you're doing dishes later y'hear?"

"Okay, but I'm not drying." John got up to cut himself some more beef.

James poured out the last of the wine into Alice and Tina's glasses, then opened the other bottle to fill his own glass up. Bill got another beer as they all very slowly finished their meals, and James wondered where John was finding room for more.

Alice told her parents about James's new venture with the website, the help and advice they were giving to folk, and they thought it was a great idea and wanted to help if they could in any way.

Once John had finally finished, James was told to make some room for dessert later, and he followed Bill over to the living room with his glass of wine, as the others cleared the table and John started doing dishes.

Bill sat with James on the couch, and keeping his voice low he spoke to him.

"Y'know James, I don't know what you've done, but you've brought our daughter back from wherever she's been for many years. Me and her mom are very grateful to you. We know what went on with her at school, at least some of it, but we could never do anything about it. Then she went to college and she came back worse, even though she got her degree. She's more alive now than we can remember, and we both think it's because of meeting you. So thank you, we are so grateful."

"It's kind of you to think that Bill, but really, I haven't done anything. I think I could just relate to what she went through and talk about it, that's all. She has been through more than what you probably realize, but she seems to be over it now, or at least I hope so."

"You're being too modest James, even Alice says it's because of you that she's feeling good. So thank you."

"Hey you guys, what you whispering about?" Shouted Alice from the kitchen as she dried dishes.

"I was trying to persuade your dad to let me see your photo albums, but he said he wanted to watch the football." Replied the smiling James.

"That's the first sensible comment he's made for years," said John, looking up from the sink.

Once all the washed dishes had been put away and Tina had fed Niner, everybody just sat around digesting their food, watching football, and making small talk.

John wanted to know how long dessert would be because he was starving. Bill had another beer and James refilled his wine glass. The others had sodas.

Alice got her brother to show her the video on his phone, gasping when the full force hit Mr. Long, then laughing before handing it to James to watch.

At the time, it had happened so quickly and with so much concentration, that James had barely taken it all in. Watching the video, he could savor it more and laughed as Mr. Long slipped and fell, then got completely covered, eventually emerging well after the truck left, like a monster from the mud. Nobody seemed to rush toward him to see if he was okay, the comments amid the laughing were about the stink coming from the pile, and then the sound of sirens as the police arrived.

Even they were reluctant to get too close. Eventually, one of them with a handkerchief over his nose and mouth, approached the stricken Mr. Long, but when a paramedic appeared, the cop made a hasty retreat. The paramedic also covered his face, and after what looked like a conversation with Mr. Long, he too made a retreat.

He did go back though, this time with a water hose that someone had set up, and he started hosing down the victim who had managed to get to his feet, but that's where the video stopped. Someone was ushering the watching audience back into school and the screen went black.

"What happened to him afterwards?" James asked John, handing back his phone.

"They said he was taken to hospital for a check up and they kept him overnight. He was released though the following day."

"He was lucky then, he could have picked up all sorts of things from being in that filth" commented the doctor Alice.

"The doctors said that the only thing that was wrong with him, was that he was full of shit," added John.

James laughed at the comment.

"Ugh" shuddered Tina, "I can only imagine."

"He's been given a new nickname at school" smiled John, and with no one asking what it was he continued, "Shitbath."

Very shortly after, Tina returned to the kitchen and asked who wanted dessert. Everyone did, so she plated them up and Alice handed them out to where they were sitting, along with a fork. A straight from the oven apple pie a la mode, and it was delicious. James wondered about having seconds, but decided not to, and the only one who could was John.

Bill was a carpenter by trade but had little work these days, his age and the recession had really hurt him. The garage was now his workshop, there was no room for a car any more, and as he didn't really have work to go to regularly, they'd sold Tina's car and she used the truck. He took James into the garage and James could appreciate his work, especially the intricate aspects.

Tina still worked part time in a hair salon and had her regular customers, which she enjoyed. It was far more of a social thing, with the women gossiping about the local goings on.

They didn't have much, but what they did have they were grateful for, and still tried to enjoy life. James wondered how they were able to feed John for seven days a week, as he always seemed to be hungry.

Tina made some coffee and everyone bar John had a cup, and Tina wanted her daughter and James to take home some of the remaining beef so that they could have a sandwich later for supper. They declined, mainly because they thought that John would probably polish it all off, or for his lunch the following day.

Alice and James departed a little while later, receiving big hugs from both parents as her brother lay prone on the couch again, and the little dog crying.

Alice took James back to his apartment. She was so happy that her family and James had gotten along so well, and that James really liked everyone, even her lazy brother.

She wanted James to follow her home, but he declined nicely, with his excuse of being just too bloated from her mother's great cooking.

She stayed there for a couple of hours, then left quietly when he began to snooze and snore a little on the couch.

This time she left him a note.

James woke up after a while and smiled reading Alice's note. He opened a bottle of Merlot and watched some television, before eventually going to his bed.

CHAPTER 27

In New York, Susan seemed to have an extra step to her stride. Business was going extremely well, her kids were doing well in school, her husband was on the up, and she was having so much fun.

The party planning aspect of her business was a great cover for her. Although her husband didn't think she needed to do it, without it, she would have needed another excuse to escape for a couple of nights each week. Having a nanny for the kids meant they were taken of, and her husband never complained when she got home in a high state of arousal. He always made sure he was awake, as it was practically a sure thing for him.

Susan wasn't the most natural mother. She loved her little children, but was only too happy to let the nanny take care of their tantrums and crying.

She'd tried at the beginning, with the diaper changing and the sleepless nights, even attempting the breast feeding. It wore her down. It made her irritable and haggard looking. She didn't like carrying the extra weight around, particularly after birth when she wanted her figure back to how it had been before. Once the second child arrived, she'd had enough, and demanded and got a great young nanny.

The money they spent on the nanny was to her mind very well spent. She did a great job with the children, and on her days off, when Susan had to deal with them, she often thought the nanny deserved double what she was paying her.

Of course, her husband Eli complained about the cost, but he never volunteered to get up in the middle of the night, or to rock them to sleep, or do anything else. Even when they were babies he never helped out, so Susan just told him to look at his own hourly rate, then compare it to the nanny and the work she had to do to get it. It usually did the trick.

Almost the whole community where they lived was Jewish. Susan didn't want to be an outcast so she had converted to the faith, and as at least a couple of the most influential members of the faith were also customers at her club, Susan's status in the community was never open to discussion.

Fridays especially were her night, either at the club or in someone's home, and it was always the highlight of her week.

Susan really liked the new employee, Candy. Like everyone Susan employed, she had done a criminal check on her. Candy had been stung once by vice for soliciting as an escort. This was to be expected, it was no surprise to Susan, she'd have been far more suspicious if her record had been clean.

Candy was working out really well. Everybody seemed to like her, nothing seemed to faze her, and no matter what the customer required, she was happy to oblige.

She'd told Susan that she still worked as an escort, as it was too well paying for her to give it up entirely. She had regular 'johns', so it was a safe environment.

Susan had also sampled Candy for herself one night, on an evening when she didn't normally go in to the club and all the customers had been early. She'd kept Candy behind after sending everyone else home, and had really enjoyed her.

Candy's only stipulation was that she didn't want to be scarred, but she'd allowed Susan to slap her, hard, and use whatever she wanted on her. Susan had a blast, it had reminded her of the time she lived with Tuesday, and she still missed those days. Susan thought she would just have to pretend to get more successful and take yet another night away from home. She knew she would never get away with being out all night, but a few hours maybe she could wrangle, or an afternoon here and there.

Susan had a small office in Greenwich Village, not far from her club. She could have used an assistant sometimes in the office, but she felt it was safer to do it all herself, and she only rarely did any respectable straight parties. So her office was really a facade, but looked real with a glass door and S. G. Party Planners stenciled onto it. There were armchairs for the customers to sit in, and to look through the many brochures, samples of cloths, silverware, glasses, and decors from the various tables.

It never raised any suspicions. After all, a party planner has to go to where the party is, but if her husband dropped by the office, or the nanny with the children, it all looked genuine.

A janitorial service went through the building five nights a week, so apart from keeping her computer and small set of files secure, she had nothing to worry about.

Most of Susan's parties were for just a handful of people. Usually it was for the people who frequented her club, who just wanted a more homier experience with their friends, or with swinger groups who were wanting to experiment. Invariably they would go much further than in the club and be less safe. Other times, it could be like what she was currently organizing, which would probably turn into a full out orgy with drugs being liberally taken.

Susan and her staff would not only be expected to participate, but also supervise and make sure no-one went too far. Susan would provide all the toys and tools, nothing very dangerous, and apart from her staff she would also provide a bar with plastic glasses. She'd once done a bar with glass and they'd been smashed everywhere. It had been a complete mess and several party goers had been cut. She would never use glass again.

It was all going to happen in a mansion in the Hampton's. It was one that the owners didn't use but rented out for weekends. Although it was furnished, it was sparse, and there weren't any antiques. Susan knew the property, she'd used it once before, so she knew exactly what was needed.

Sheets were required to cover everything, and everywhere. Cheap sheets that could be thrown away afterward, so she generally bought decorator's that were huge and not expensive. They were perfect for all the bodily fluids and spilled drinks. Without sheets, Susan knew there would be very many stains to clean up that would take time and much effort.

Susan didn't normally do food catering, but for this party she would order snacks, fruits, ice creams and whipped creams, and have them delivered early in the day.

She would also buy towels by the dozen, lubricants, toilet rolls, soaps, band aids, porn movies, tampons, and condoms. Susan had rules regarding her staff, and she had to protect them.

As most of her clientele would be attending this party, Susan would close the club for the night. She didn't have an exact number of how many were attending, but it was already in three figures. Those who weren't into S & M were being told to wear fancy dress of their choosing, but with a sexual element.

As far as music was concerned, the one thing the house had was a piano. Not a great piano, or even a well preserved one, but a piano all the same. Susan knew a pianist who not only could tune it, but he was also not averse to crazy things happening around him.

Susan liked these parties. They didn't occur often, or regularly, but when they did, they were wild, sexy, and chaotic.

She wouldn't tell her staff where the party was, she never did, but she would have to give them some warning about it, as they tended to last for a long time, and she would also have to make an excuse to be away from home.

CHAPTER 28

James heard about the party not very long after Candy had been told about it. She was asked if she wanted to participate, what it would entail, and the price being paid to her, before she accepted.

James had already done much work and research on Susan Ward, but this news was exciting. Although he'd found both her and her business, her family and social standing, she was careful enough to not open emails from people she didn't know, or attachments. James had tried sending several from bogus businesses in hopes of getting into her computer, but she hadn't opened one of them.

He was now trying the online S & M clubs in New York, which Susan would no doubt be aware of, and most probably even be a member of one or more of them. To organize a big party, they would have to be a part of some club. It's not like they could put flyers on telegraph poles to advertise it. He eventually got a hit.

The party was by invitation only, no location was given or when it was going to be, just that everyone was being checked and vetted. If you weren't known or not vouched for, then you didn't get invited. James wasn't worried about that, he wasn't after an invitation, he just wanted to hack into the system for the information.

Once he got the email address of who to contact, James sent a message. He'd worked for a long time putting his attachment together, but if the short message on the actual email didn't make them open it, then he would have to keep composing different messages until one did. Fortunately, it worked first time.

He said he was from an S & M group in Miami, and mentioned names he'd found. The attachment was his fake personal details and the names of people who would vouch for him.

The reply he got from the club expressed regret, but they had already reached their limit for this particular party. However, they would keep his details, as they were in the process of arranging another party as there was so much interest, and that he would hear back from them very soon.

James was in.

The online club tried to protect their members as far as possible. The emails they sent to their members looked very innocent, and would raise no suspicions if someone else happened to see them, at work or at home.

The online club was free, so no membership fees could be traced, but James was able to retrieve all the email addresses of the members. The club had many advertisers, which no doubt paid their overheads and more, and they did reviews of sex toys and clubs, their prices and specialities.

From what James could discover, the club had recommended the house they were going to use, but all the costs for the party were being paid through Susan's business. Everyone was given links to a website, and a different link to pay their fee. If, for any reason they needed a receipt, then they needed to ask for one.

The party itself was being described in correspondence as a special shareholders meeting, with full participation.

The website itself gave the general information for the party and the rules. It was $500 per person. Refreshments were included. Parking was limited so there would be a remote location to park in, not far away, with a limo shuttle service to the house. There would be a changing area at the house if required, but attendees were advised to leave purses and wallets in their cars, which would be kept secure.

No unauthorized guests would be admitted. Everyone would have to check in, but to protect their identities, they would be given a unique number on payment. If they lost their number, or couldn't remember it, there would be no admittance. No cameras. No phones. No videos

Payment would only be received from members of the online club who had been granted permission to attend.

If anyone had a STD, then under no circumstance were they to have unprotected sex, and if they were found to have flaunted the rule, any current membership of an S & M club would be revoked for life. They would also be blacklisted from joining one in the entire country.

On clicking the payment link, after verification and payment, the attendees would be given a map to the remote location, the time to be there, and their unique admittance numbers.

James investigated the link, and it looked like a business supply company. Very clever. He already knew from going through the correspondence that Susan Ward was the main point of payments, but he'd thought she would just use the party planning side. He guessed this bogus supply company was to avoid questions from uninvolved partners, about why there was a payment to a party planner.

The club was sending attachments to Susan of the accepted attendees, so James was able to place his tiny bug on one. The information inside Susan's computer was amazing, and James made full use of it.

Elsewhere, James was discovering that very many adults were having huge problems with bullies, mainly at work, but also at home. James was trying to point them towards the right kind of help with the links on his webpage, but it was very difficult for these people. Naming people when you're an adult is much harder than when you're a child, as the repercussions can be catastrophic. The economy was such, that to lose your job for complaining about someone wasn't something that anyone wanted to contemplate. Finding another job was nigh on impossible.

Most of the messages James was getting from his growing website was from folk who just wanted to be heard. Very often, the bullied feel alone and helpless, so just hearing other stories makes them feel a little better. It was heart wrenching for James to read. Women fearful of their husband's coming home, grown men forced to give up their weekends and vacations because of excessive demands from employers, people forced out of necessity to take jobs that paid the absolute minimum with no benefits. Then there were the folk being chased and harassed by debt collectors for mainly medical bills, that they had no hope of paying. It was just awful.

Banks were still foreclosing, families were finding their houses were now worth a lot less than they'd paid for them, yet folk were still demanding money from them that they didn't have.

James was so busy with the website and the research he was doing, he resolved to take up Alice's parents offer and have them help with the website.

He hadn't seen a great deal of Alice lately, he'd wanted to, but he'd just been taken aback by the traffic to the website, and it was only the beginning.

He talked to her about the website on one of the nights he went over. She was fully supportive of what he was trying to do, she just wanted to be with him more, and she thought her parents were sincere in their offer to help out.

Alice did wonder, just as James did, how big the website was going to get and what then?

James thought he would then have it professionally hosted and managed, with councilors answering the messages rather than himself, who didn't really know how to respond to some of them.

James also thought he could do a list of the good employers, after checking, versus the bad employers. James figured that the good employers would like to be known, and would pay a sum to be on the list and advertise. That would help pay for the website, the professional help, and contribute to the various agencies that James was sending people to.

James told Alice about the folk who were being mistreated at work, and she suggested they not only document their own experiences, but also others. That way the bosses wouldn't be able to pinpoint a particular person who was complaining and fire them. A ton of complaints and bad press would surely force a rethink on the owners part.

Alice thought they should go to Sunday lunch again at her parents house, ask them to help, get their thoughts on the whole issue, and talk about where it was all heading.

CHAPTER 29

Donny White took his time going home after work, and as he also had to pick up some groceries on his way, he roamed the familiar supermarket aisles as if he had all the time in the world.

Despite Donny having a very well paid job, a beautiful wife, an expensive home in a good neighborhood, and a great car to drive, he was miserable. He didn't think anyone, even if they had nothing compared to him, could be as unhappy as himself.

As Donny paused with his shopping cart on seeing his reflection in a security mirror at the end of an aisle, he saw the man he'd become, and he didn't like him. It seemed that nobody liked him anymore, apart from his dog, Gina.

Donny had always been shy and withdrawn, keeping to himself most of the time, and not attracting the wrong kind of attention. He'd always been nerdy, and his friends through school and college had been the same way. Donny had lost touch with his former friends over the years, so he felt really alone these days. Even his own family seemed like strangers when he was allowed to see them, and Donny sometimes thought that they must really dislike him.

At school, Donny hadn't looked like a nerd like his friends. He'd been quite a handsome boy with his short blonde hair and good features. He'd had girlfriends aplenty, but he had only felt really comfortable with the girls who were also nerdy, his shyness never seeming to work with the partying schoolgirls.

It had been different with Julie, his wife who he'd met at college. She wasn't at all interested in parties, nor computers, apart from using the social media side of them. She had stuck with him, married him, and was now waiting for him at home. A home he didn't want to go back to.

Donny worked for an electronics company as a software designer, which he liked doing, but it hadn't worked out as expected. The promotions had never materialized, and the new supervisor, who was just out of college, was making things even worse.

Donny had always felt like an outsider at work. He was never included in other's social events, and everyone seemed to whisper to each other whenever he was in earshot. He'd never been too bothered by not being invited anywhere, he wouldn't have been able to go anyway, but the former supervisor at least, was kind to him. She tried telling him he had to be more outgoing to achieve advancement, but that his work was exemplary, and she would help him move up the ladder.

Then she was gone. Apparently because of her reluctance to approve products that weren't ready. She was replaced by a young guy who was giving Donny bigger workloads, shorter deadlines, and then giving Donny poor evaluations. The other workers were making shortcuts and lowering the quality of the products, but Donny couldn't let himself do that, and he was being made to pay.

It was plainly obvious the new supervisor was trying to force Donny out, but as Donny always got his work done and made the ridiculous deadlines, he couldn't fire him, and he had no other reason to get rid of him.

Although the products were selling well, Donny was noticing the complaints were steadily increasing about the poor quality of the newer products, compared to how they used to be. Once they were reliable with very high ratings.

So Donny put up with it, ignoring the accusations of purposely making mistakes, being lied to, or being shut down when he offered an opinion.

It was a casual wearing workplace, almost everyone wore jeans and tee shirts. Donny had never fitted in. He was always sent to work in a short sleeved dress shirt, with a tie, slacks, a patterned sweater, his blond hair combed with a parting down the middle of his scalp, and huge eyeglasses. Donny had been wearing variations of this outfit for so long he'd gotten used to it. Julie said she liked him like this.

As Donny continued shopping, he was heard answering his cell phone.

"Yes dear, I'm in the store. I'll be home shortly. I know you're hungry. Yes, I've got the wine you like."

Donny made his way home after checking out and loading the trunk of his Range Rover with the groceries and wine he'd bought.

The house he shared with Julie was a large two level home in a gated community. The whole neighborhood was maintained by a landscaping crew which was paid by the yearly dues, along with the security firm that kept away the solicitors and the uninvited. The swimming pool was looked after by a company that also served some of the neighbors, but as it was a salt water pool, it wasn't labor intensive. Julie had always wanted a home with a pool, to her it was a necessity.

Donny pulled into the double garage and parked alongside his wife's Jaguar. Gathering the grocery bags out of the trunk, he headed to the door that led into the kitchen, hitting the garage door opener before opening the door.

Gina was waiting for him as usual, and he had to put down the bags to greet her.

She was a huge St. Bernard that Donny adored, but Julie was getting tired of because of her size. When they got her, Julie thought it was fashionable to have a large dog, and Donny had just fallen in love with her at first sight. He didn't even mind her slobbering, or her clumsiness when she was a puppy, but Julie almost instantly complained about it. If not for Donny looking after her, Julie would have got rid of her a long time ago. The housekeeper liked her as well, so between them they kept Gina out of the way.

Gina leapt at Donny with total happiness, covering Donny with her saliva, fur, and wet licks. She towered over Donny when she got on her hind legs, and it took all his strength to stop her from toppling him over. It was the only part of the day that Donny ever looked forward to.

Once Gina's excitement abated, Donny re-gathered the shopping bags and deposited them on the large kitchen island. Jonelle, the housekeeper, had left Donny a note to say that she'd prepared dinner and what to do with it after getting it out of the fridge. To Donny, Jonelle was a life saver.

Gina was dancing around, so Donny fed her before putting away the groceries and going through to the family room to let Julie know he was home.

Julie was watching one of her soap operas from the huge couch in front of the big screen TV. A glass of red wine was beside her, as she sat elegantly with her legs crossed and her back ramrod straight. Her long blonde hair was set in its usual bun, her skin tanned from the sessions on the sun bed, nails long and manicured, the fingers adorned with large rings.

She was dressed this night in black Capri pants, and a sleeveless blouse in white with frilly lace covering her breasts. Julie had her full make up on. Donny could barely remember the last time he'd seen her au natural, as it seemed she was always expecting visitors.

"I'm home," he announced.

"You took your sweet time" Julie admonished, "I suppose you were ogling all the horny housewives in the store."

"No I wasn't, they were slow on the checkout. I came home as fast as I could."

"Like everything else Donny, you're a poor liar. Give me the receipt and get my dinner. While you've been dallying around, I've been waiting here for you. This is the last glass of wine so you'd better have got some more. Now go and get my dinner and keep that disgusting dog away from me." Julie told him, not even glancing in his direction.

Donny handed over the receipt which Julie just snatched away.

Julie didn't eat with Donny anymore unless they were out somewhere, so he followed the directions Jonelle had left, and prepared the tray for Julie.

Taking it to the family room, he put the tray on a small portable table and put it in front of Julie who was still engrossed in her show. He'd also brought one of the bottles of wine he'd bought, and he put it on her tray after refilling her glass. He was hoping she hadn't drunk too much before he arrived, as he made a hasty retreat back to the kitchen.

Donny ate his meal with Gina as his company, watching the local news on the small television in the kitchen. There wasn't much news, but the dinner was good and he handed some morsels to the grateful Gina.

After Donny put his own plates in the dishwasher, he retrieved Julie's which was only half eaten. That was normal for her, but she made up for it with the amount of wine she drank, and Donny noticed that she had refilled her glass from the bottle he'd brought.

"Your mother called earlier," Julie informed him. "She wouldn't tell me what she wanted but she wants you to call her back. I don't know why she wants to talk to you, it's not like you ever have anything interesting to say. I blame her for the way you are, you're just too soft to ever make anything of yourself. If it wasn't for me, you'd still be living with her and playing with yourself in the garage. Give me your phone, I want to see who you've been calling all day long because you certainly haven't called me. You can call your bitch of a mother when you've done the dishes." Julie hadn't even glanced in Donny's direction as she spoke to him in her usual disdainful way.

Donny returned to the kitchen to clean up the rest of the dishes, and to turn on the dishwasher before returning to the family room. Gina knew better than to try to follow her master, so she lay down in her bed to await his return.

Julie's program had finished so she had muted the television, and she handed the cell phone back to Donny. She was standing now, a glass in one hand and the other on her hip with her back to the unlit fireplace.

"I'm sure you have another phone somewhere, even someone as boring as yourself gets calls. Probably from your mother so she can talk to you behind my back. If I ever find out she's been talking to you on this phone, or the one you have stashed away somewhere, there'll be hell to pay. Now call that mother of yours while I have time to listen, and put it on speaker. I want to hear what bad things she'll say about me this time."

"Hi mom, how are you?" Donny asked as his mother answered her phone, and he put it on speaker as Julie waved an angry finger at him.

"I'm good Donny, we're just worried about you is all. Is everything okay with you?" She asked in her pleasant but worried voice.

"Everything is fine mom."

"Am I on speaker again?" His mom asked.

"Yes, I'm working on a broken computer." Donny lied.

"Julie is listening isn't she? Why can I never have a private conversation with you Donny? Is that too much to ask? You never answer your phone during the day, is that because you're not allowed to? I bet Julie doesn't let you listen in on her conversations. A pity she doesn't, you might learn something from her calls."

Donny could see that Julie was fuming, and getting her in a bad mood was never a good thing to do.

"Julie isn't here mom, it's just me." Donny replied, not answering any of the questions.

"There's no need to lie to me Donny. I know she won't let you talk to any of your family without her being around, and listening to everything we say. So is she pregnant yet, or still as barren and cold as she's always been?"

"No, Julie isn't pregnant yet mom. She's not as bad as you think she is."

"Well lets see if she allows you to come home for an hour or two this weekend. We need to discuss a private family matter with you Donny."

"What matter mom? Julie is family now so she has to be included."

"This has nothing to do with Julie. She can go and get her nails manicured again, or do a bit of work for once in her life. Even cook you a meal if she knows where the stove is."

"Mom, you know that Julie doesn't need to work. I make plenty of money for us both. We've been through this before."

"It still needs to be said Donny. She doesn't lift a finger to help you. She's more concerned about strutting her fanny around town than she is about you. So ask her if you can come over for a couple of hours, and if you don't show up I'll know what her answer was."

"Okay mom, I'll see you at the weekend. Okay?"

"All right Donny, I hope so. I love you."

"I love you too mom."

When Donny hung up, Julie went into a rage. Her empty wine glass was hurled in Donny's direction, and he had to duck to avoid it before it smashed into the wall behind him.

"There is no way in hell that you are going to your Mother's without me. I have no intention of ever going there unless it's with my gun, and I shoot the lot of you. I am serious Donny. I have had it up to here with you and your damn family. If I ever hear, or even suspect that you have been talking to them behind my back, you'd all better watch out. That dog of yours will be first, followed by your no good family, and then you. I am not kidding you Donny. You're nothing without me, so you do as I say. You hear me!" Julie bellowed.

"I hear you Julie. Don't worry, I'm not going to mom's nor will I talk behind your back. I'm sorry for what mom said, I'm sure she didn't mean it." Donny said, softly.

"Oh she meant it. She knew I was here listening. She'll be sorry when I go over there and blast her with my .38. She knows I have one doesn't she?"

"I don't think so."

"Well you do, and I am not afraid of using it. Now get out of my sight for a while and take that dog out. I'll keep your phone with me. We are having sex later so take a shower. I don't want your smelly sweat all over me. Now go!"

Donny made a hasty retreat, and after putting the leash on Gina he took her for a long walk, dreading having to have sex with his wife.

He used to like going to bed with Julie when she was loving and fun. As the years passed, she had not only moved Donny out of the bedroom because she said he was always disturbing her sleep, but she always complained about his stamina, his small manhood, or not doing things right. It had gotten to the stage where she did very little to arouse him, yet Donny was expected to satisfy her, mainly with a vibrator, and to wear a condom when she eventually wanted him inside her.

It had been so different in the beginning, but Donny felt increasingly inadequate as time went by.

As for children, Donny knew that would never happen, but he was glad about that now. He'd wanted them when they got married, but his paternal instincts had gradually diminished. He just couldn't imagine Julie as a Mother.

When Donny finally returned to the house and deposited Gina temporarily in the kitchen, he went to his room and took a shower and a shave. Julie disliked rough skin. After putting on her favorite after shave and deodorant, he waited for her, naked beneath his sheets.

It was two hours before she'd had her fill of Donny and had retired to her own bed. Donny was sore from having his face slapped, his hair pulled. It had been angry sex and in no way did he feel satisfied or content.

Only after he'd retrieved Gina and she'd bounded onto his bed did he feel even remotely happy, and he fell asleep with his arm around his dog, who quietly snored beside him.

It was at work the following day, during his lunch period, that Donny happened across James's website.

Donny had never thought he was the victim of a bully, that only happened to kids, and he was sure that he'd never been bullied at school. As he kept reading, he discovered that adults were victims as much as children, and it wasn't only at the hands of males. There were very many female bullies, and it was hard for men to stand up to them without resorting to violence, which would result in the man being arrested. It was a terrible scenario. Most people couldn't understand the notion of a man being bullied by his wife, and it was very degrading to admit to it. As Donny read more stories, husbands being belittled by their wives in public, being laughed at and abused in the most intimate way, he realized he wasn't alone. Donny's biggest worry though, was Julie's threats towards his family and pet. He had no doubt in his mind that she would harm them, and that was his biggest fear. She had nothing without Donny, he gave her everything she had, and she wouldn't give up her life without a hell of a fight.

Donny sent an email to James's website.

After reading many of your stories, my own may seem trivial, but to myself it feels horrendous.

Being a grown man, with a very well paying job, a large house, two expensive cars, an attractive wife and no money worries at all, you may well think I have it all. What can I complain about?

Truth be told, I've allowed myself to get into this mess, and I feel just as bullied as those poor children and women. I don't know how to stop it. Although work is my escape, it's also another hell, with being constantly ignored, being given the bigger workloads, harsher demands, and no advancements. Since the new supervisor took over, no raises have been awarded to me, and he refuses to credit me for any of my ideas that he uses, pretending they are all his own. It's home that's the biggest problem though. My wife has developed a violent streak, mocks and abuses me, drinks too much, doesn't cook or grocery shop, hates my dog, and threatens to kill all my side of the family. She doesn't allow me to do anything alone, listens to and checks the numbers on my cell phone, and reads all my mail. I don't even have a door key to my own house.

I am so fearful of what she will do if I don't go home. She has a gun, knows how to use it, and she knows where I work and where my family live.

If you are able, please advise.

James recognized the company name that was attached to the email and was a little surprised but not shocked. Micro management seemed to be happening everywhere, except where it should be. To the administers. It was the perfect way to deny someone a decent raise, make them work even harder and longer, which then paved the way for heftier bonuses for those at the top.

James sent a quick reply back, telling Donny to call the enclosed telephone number the following day at lunchtime, after buying a prepaid phone.

For the first time in years, Donny suddenly felt a little hopeful. He didn't even care if someone reported him for sending personal email, knowing the company had someone check all outgoing emails, and employees Facebook pages.

When he arrived home, Donny took in that Julie's car space was vacant and Jonelle was waiting for him in the kitchen, sitting at the kitchen island with a glass of iced tea.

"Hi Jonelle, it's good to see you," Donny said in obvious delight, "I rarely get to see you these days."

Gina had already met her master in the garage, had even tried climbing over him into the car, but now she had calmed down a little as Donny scratched the back of her ears.

"That ain't my fault Sir, I just do as the lady tells me," Jonelle replied in her flat southern voice.

Jonelle was a strong, tall black woman who was a great cook and housekeeper. She kept her mouth and opinions, did her work, and went home. Although she always came to work in unflattering, one piece, brown work dresses, her straightened hair tightly pinned back, Donny thought that with her strong features she would be a knockout when she got dressed up.

"So is something wrong Jonelle? Do you need my help with anything?" Donny never even gave a thought that something may have happened to Julie.

"No Sir, nothing to worry about. I just wanted you to know that your wife is at one of her friends, some party or other, but would be home later. She didn't give a time, just said for you to leave the lights on in the garage.

Your dinner is in the oven Sir, it will be ready in ten minutes, and now I'll go home."

Jonelle got up and put her glass in the dishwasher, put on her coat, and picked up her bag.

"How are your family Jonelle? I never hear anything anymore. Are they all doing well?"

"I believe you were the last one in this house to ask me that Sir, so thank you. Yes, they are doing just fine. They often ask about you and they missed seeing you when you weren't able to come to a few things. I must go now Sir, but you take good care of yourself, y'hear?"

"I hear you Jonelle and say hi to everyone. Do you need a ride?"

"I'm parked around the corner Sir, is all. Goodnight."

Julie hadn't liked it once, when Jonelle had arrived to work in a battered old car, so she told her to park around the corner. Jonelle had continued to do this, despite what car she drove, and Julie had never told her to park in front of the house again.

Donny had no idea that he'd been invited to anything to do with Jonelle's family.

He spent a relaxing night with Gina, totally enjoyed the baked chicken that had been left for him, and a few glasses of wine as he watched a movie in his room.

Donny left a few minutes earlier for work the following morning. He hadn't checked during the night to see if Julie had returned home, he didn't care anymore. Her car wasn't in the garage when he pulled out, but he paid no heed, he wanted to get his prepaid phone.

James detected the hope, desperation, and helplessness in Donny's voice when he called. It takes a lot for an adult male to confess that he's being victimized by a smaller woman, but if you're a gentleman, it's very difficult to fight back.

James thought that Donny needed to get away from his existence quickly, and told Donny so, who agreed but didn't know how to, or if his family would be safe.

Although Donny had siblings, they were on the other side of the country, so it was really just his mother and father who were nearby. They were both retired.

James hadn't given his real name to Donny, but asked him for his complete trust despite being a total stranger. Donny gave it, and James asked for all his financial details, along with an introduction to his parents. After Donny told James everything about his finances, or at least what he knew as Julie had taken them over, he called his parents and they had a three way call. Donny's parents seemed very pleasant and only too glad to help.

James asked them if they knew a divorce lawyer, but they didn't, which seemed to deflate them a little, but once he told them it didn't matter, that he would find one, they improved a little.

"Listen to me everyone," James confidently spoke. "We all believe that Donny needs to get out of his environment very quickly. I think that should be by tomorrow morning at the latest. Now, in the morning, Donny will need to sign papers to set in motion the divorce proceedings, and sign a restraining order. Once he does that, I think you should all go away for a few days. I don't think Julie will start shooting, but you never know, so I think it's best you disappear and she gets hit with a lawyer. I will make sure she can't do much with your finances Donny. Can you get away by the morning?"

"What about my job, my dog, and where could we go?" Said the suddenly doubtful Donny.

"Apart from the job, we have the perfect answer son," proclaimed the previously quiet father, "we have an R.V. We can go on a road trip."

"This is why I married you honey," answered his wife. "We'll be ready to roll first thing in the morning after we stock up and fill the gas tank."

"Then that's the plan Donny," interjected James. "Don't worry about your job. I know someone in your line that will give you work, and I will tell your current employers why you're going. Don't say anything to anyone. Go home as normal, and put together your essential stuff, that you can quietly sneak away. Keep the prepaid phone hidden and turned off, and if something unexpected happens that you need to talk about, call me as soon as you can. Now let me have your parents address for the lawyer, and just try to stay as normal as possible. Okay?"

Donny gave his okay and the address, before the phone went dead with everyone going their separate ways.

Rather than excitement, Donny only showed worry, which raised no alarm bells whatsoever at work or at home.

Julie did not mention where she'd been all night when Donny got home, she acted as if she hadn't been away from home at all, and was exactly the same, if not worse, than normal. Donny didn't care where she'd been, and if she'd been with a man, good luck to him.

She wanted to know why he was late, to look at his phone to see who he'd called, check his messages, asked where her dinner was, and needed more wine. She also had more to say about Donny's lack of manhood, and that if he was a real man, he would ravage her every night with no inhibitions.

Donny gave her more wine than normal that night. Julie wasn't a good drunk and her abuse of him got louder and more profound as the evening wore on. Donny usually avoided these outbursts like the plague, but he knew that eventually it would stop, and she would go to bed, falling into a very deep sleep that would keep her in bed until mid morning.

When her bedroom door slammed shut, he started putting his things together and loading up the range rover. Gina was well aware something was going on, she had a major sulk going on as she watched from her lying position on Donny's bed. If she'd seen him collecting her food, toys, feeding bowls and pills, she wouldn't have been so worried, as she watched the bags being filled and hangars taken out of the closet.

Donny had no intention of taking all of his things on a road journey, he'd separated everything so that he could just put most of it in his parents house.

It was almost light before Donny was done. He hadn't been to sleep and he drank some welcoming coffee, before taking his regular shower and getting dressed.

He then took the still worried Gina for a very quick walk, before taking her back into the quiet kitchen. Donny had written Jonelle a small note, so left it a place that Julie would never look, in her cleaning bucket. Gina couldn't figure out where her water bowl was, but after Donny took a quick look around and called her, she bounded after him and leapt happily into the running car. Donny leaned across her to close the passenger door.

The lawyer, along with a sheriff's deputy, arrived for the signatures just as Donny had stored his belongings and was making himself at home in the fifth wheel. The deputy would serve the restraining order. To Donny, the lawyer looked sharp and nasty, the deputy too big to mess with. He could only imagine the look on Julie's face when she was faced by these two.

The R.V. was a luxurious motor home that was the size of a bus. Donny's parents had hitched their car onto the back of it, and so Donny parked his Range Rover in their garage. Gina thought it was all fun, and after Donny signed and initialed the documents in all the highlighted spaces, he went and lay down on the bed as Gina rode up front, to see where they were heading.

James had taken away Julie's ability to do what she wanted with Donny's and her finances. He'd reversed her own actions with Donny, and now it would be her with restricted funds, with no way of changing it. She wouldn't be able to do anything without Donny's approval anymore, or until after the divorce.

James also made a couple of calls to find Donny another job in a friendlier environment, and after finding success there, he made another call to the owner of Donny's previous company to tell them he would not be returning there, that they were forsaking quality for production, but good luck to them for the short term.

James had been happy to help out Donny. It hadn't taken much on his part and Donny was a decent guy who'd been too trusting.

CHAPTER 30

After making up a story about having to attend an AGM and Conference, James eventually flew to New York armed with yet more electronics and devices, his laptop, and the information about Susan Ward.

He found a hotel, that coincidentally was having a shareholders conference, with a room available. It was very expensive but served the purpose. He also got a great view of Central Park.

After renting a small box truck, he bought some camping supplies and set the back of the truck up with his electronics, and enough gear for a night away from the hotel. He checked it one night while it was in the hotel's car park, to make sure that any lights from inside the truck couldn't be seen. After a couple of modifications, he was happy with it.

With all the information he'd garnered from Susan's computer, he wanted to get real photos of some of the people who were attending the party, even some who weren't, but that he knew were influential people and would be very embarrassed by being members of an S & M club.

He hadn't known any of the names at first, but after researching he recalled that he had heard of some of them, and the rest he learned about. It was very interesting to learn that some of these people, who publicly had certain views, and weren't shy in proclaiming them, didn't live by them privately.

The truck, like most vehicles in New York, was next to useless in the city, so James acted like a regular tourist, using the subway, cabs, and taking pictures of everything with his phone, including the unsuspecting party goers and club members.

James spent many hours on the streets doing this, sometimes having to wait for long periods before his targets showed themselves. Wherever possible, and it was the main reason for doing this, he would get them climbing into a vehicle that wasn't a cab, and had a license plate.

In between doing this, he went one day to the party house and the car park, to set up his equipment. Going during the day to avoid suspicion. Setting up, and the clean up, was the most dangerous task for him.

The car park being used for the party was by day a public car park for beach goers. At night, it was usually empty, but if there were cars then people would assume that there was a beach party. James had also found out that sometimes residents used it as a guest parking spot, and there was a fee that Susan had paid to facilitate this.

James set up tiny cameras that would cover any vehicles, and their license plates, entering or leaving, and as they didn't have any tell tale red lights on them, they would be extremely hard to spot.

After doing that, not being noticed by anyone who'd left their car in the lot to go swimming, James drove down to the house.

He resolved to himself that if he came across anybody, then he would simply tell them he'd made a wrong turn and would leave. If he was inside the house and someone came, then he would quickly get outside and ask if it was for sale or for rent.

James had seen the house on its own website, so he knew it was big and what he needed equipment wise, but it was still a shock to him when it appeared in his windscreen. It was huge. From the air it would look like a capital H, with the wings on one side enclosing the entrance at the front and at the back the swimming pool.

James took the circular drive to the front door and parked directly outside, looking for security cameras all the way. The website hadn't mentioned any, but the owners may have had some for their own peace of mind, so he had to check.

Not seeing any, he inspected the front door, looking around and upwards to find any alarm boxes or an ad to promote the security company. He did find a box, high up on one of the walls, and the name was discernible, so he went back to his truck for his tools, and to look up the alarm company.

There were full length windows by the side of the big front door, so once James had his tools he looked through them to try to find the alarm control pad. He needed to get to it quickly, otherwise he could well be screwed.

The front door was easy, but before opening it and setting off the time delay, he checked the gadget in his hand along with the tools he would need to deal with the alarm pad. Taking a deep breath, he opened the door quickly, and stepping inside he was looking around the walls, searching for the alarm pad.

Only problem was, there was no beeping sound to be heard. Nothing. Just an eerie silence.

Running around, trying to find the alarm pad, James panicked as he frantically searched, opening doors to closets and looking behind drapes for the elusive control box. Giving in and returning to the front door, expecting the bells and whistles to go off, he inspected the front door and looked around the vast entry hall and its grand staircase for sensors. There were no sensors, and the door jamb had no pads. The house had no alarm. It was just a fake alarm box to deter opportunistic thieves.

After giving a huge sigh of relief, James got his equipment from the truck and with his already prepared small map of the house, he set about placing his cameras. Most of the cameras were hidden in everyday household objects like carriage clocks, alarm clocks, light bulbs, and smoke sensors. Others would be easily hidden in corners and in shadows.

James figured that most attendees would probably be masked, and he wanted to try to catch them unmasked. The bathrooms were his main target, as he thought they would remove any face coverings to wash up. So he especially wanted to catch the mirrors with his cameras.

The formal dining room was at the rear of the main house, alongside the huge kitchen and panty, and James thought that as the room was just a long table with chairs, it would be the perfect place for the folk to change, or to leave their clothing in if they used the bathrooms to change in. A clock on the fireplace would raise no suspicions.

There were so many rooms, James had to keep checking his map. Eight bedrooms, twelve bathrooms, billiards room, library, morning room, drawing room, family room in the huge basement, pool changing room, staff break room, butler's pantry, movie theater, gym, conservatory, nanny's quarters, house office. There was also an indoor pool in the basement, along with a spa and a sauna. It was massive.

Once James was satisfied with the positioning of his cameras, some with audio, he left the main house and closed and locked the front door. He didn't know how much time he had so he didn't want to push it, so he just trusted his judgement with the positioning of the cameras.

James then moved his truck before walking around to the back of the house to cover the outdoor pool.

He hadn't seen a soul around the house as he placed his cameras, so he made a leisurely retreat back to the car park. Once parked, he went into the back of his truck and activated the cameras, to make sure he was getting the pictures. He knew he was well within the range, but he needed to check for any issues. He had four screens with multi views, and another screen that he could use for a single feed from any of the cameras. Everything was set up to record, so if he missed something useful at the time, he would be able to go back to it later. After editing, he'd have a movie, or maybe two.

A couple of the cameras weren't positioned as correctly as he thought, but he passed it off. He didn't want to return to the house to alter them, they would have to do.

After turning off the equipment, James did one more thing before leaving for the day. He'd noticed on a couple of the parked cars that they had some kind of permit for the car park, so after watching a couple leave, he investigated.

It seemed that the local people had a resident permit that allowed them unrestricted access to the car park and beach at any time. James returned to his truck for a tool, then stole one from one of the cars before leaving.

CHAPTER 31

On the day of the party, Susan and all her staff arrived early at the house. The limo driver she always used, who was also a customer on his times off, had found another driver who he trusted, and he'd been able to get a couple of limo buses for the evening. The driver had been delivering the supplies in the afternoon, and Susan and her crew started to set up everything when they arrived.

Everyone had a specific job. Either covering everything with sheets, distributing the towels, setting up the bar, placement of toys and condoms, putting the food in the fridges, and all of them getting their bearings. One of the girls was in charge of greeting and checking, and everyone had been told to enjoy themselves, keep an eye on everything, and under no circumstances were they to have unprotected sex if they wanted to indulge. There was no pressure to do so, it was up to them.

The pianist had travelled to the house with them, so he was busy tuning the piano, which was driving everyone crazy with the monotonous single notes he was playing. Like the others, he was already dressed for the evening in his leather costume.

One of Susan's guys was good with electronics, so he was putting on the movies in a continuous loop, and although he was keeping the noise level down so as not to drown out the pianist, you could still hear the fake moans of the participants.

Everything was ready quite quickly. Susan went around checking, dimming lights, adjusting sheets, moving toys around.

She felt very sexy and horny tonight. Her thigh level stiletto heeled shoes left an enticing bare patch of skin between the boots and her costume, that had a zip all the way to her crutch. Her gloves came to above her elbows, which left another bare patch of skin before meeting her sleeveless one piece, which was a soft and thin black leather. Her hair was down tonight, but she wore an eye mask over her heavy mascaraed eyes. Her lips were a vivid red, and she toted a coiled whip.

Like the others, she'd changed at the club, and now was enjoying a plastic glass of champagne, as everyone waited for the guests to arrive.

They didn't have to wait long and soon there was a line at the door as they checked in with their numbers, some going to change in the dining room as groups of others were taken on a quick tour of the house, before being left to their own devices.

James had parked in a corner of the lot long before anyone arrived, and he not only had the permit on his windscreen, but also a for sale sign with a bogus telephone number.

The back of the truck was very cozy with all the screens, a camp chair, and a sleeping bag. He also had food and drink, and a very large bottle with bleach in it, so that he could pee if he needed to without stepping out of the truck.

James had been calling Alice every day since arriving in New York, and he couldn't wait to return home, but he wondered what she would make of all this.

He watched all the cars arrive and the occupants get into the limos, amazed at how most of them were dressed in their tight, revealing, leather or Lycra costumes. The main color was black, but others were in red, purple, pink, yellow, and even white. A few others, women, were in fancy dress, but even then it was sexy lingerie, stockings with garters, mini skirts, low cut period bodice dresses, school uniforms, and one woman in an almost there wonder woman costume.

The ages of the participants varied from early twenties to up to around seventy years of age, but the oldest woman that James saw was around fifty, and she had a great figure. Most of the women did, and it surprised James that they liked this kind of scene.

After the last car arrived and the occupants were whisked away, the two limos returned to the car park and the drivers wandered around, before they sat and waited in one of the busses. James had watched them on the screen as they came up to his truck, looking at his permit in the windscreen before moving off. After they went and relaxed in the bus, he donned the headphones to listen to some of the audio, watching the screens, incredulous at the antics going on.

It had seemed to start in the basement, with two couples who were having group sex, removing parts of their costumes as they intermingled. Very soon, there seemed to be goings on everywhere,

151

men on men, women on women, men on women, and folk being whipped, paddled, slapped, clamped and handcuffed. One or two had chains around their necks and they were being pulled along on all fours. No sooner had they finished with one or more partners, they moved on to others. Under his headphones James could hear groans, screams and yelling, but also the piano playing standard tunes.

As the pianist played, one woman was giving him a blow job while a couple cavorted on the piano itself. James wondered how he was able to stay in tune.

James had kept an eye on Susan since she'd first arrived, mask less, and who he recognized from a photo on her computer. The way that she acted, she was obviously in charge, and the whip she held made him think of Alice. Susan had been going from room to room, wearing her mask since the party goers arrived, sometimes watching, other times getting heavily involved.

Many of the participants took drugs of some kind in the bathrooms before returning to the party. James couldn't tell what they were taking, but suspected cocaine, and a good amount of Viagra. People also ate and drank copiously when they took breathers, before going to different rooms and other partners.

James didn't know Candy and had never met her. Crystal had said she was beautiful and had short, spiky red hair, but that was all. There were three or four women with red hair, but only one with spiky. Even with her mask on James could tell she was good looking, but many of the women were. Beautiful and slim. Some of the things they were doing, or being subjected to, didn't look very pleasurable to James. It was shocking to him to see the utmost joy that they expressed from receiving pain, giving it, and having multiple partners of both sexes.

Candy, if it was her, seemed to be having a blast with both men and women. It didn't seem to matter to her, but Susan only seemed to like being with women. She was more vigorous and animated with them. She'd whipped the men, hard, and although she did the same with the women, it seemed to be with a little less vigor. Not much, just not as forceful. It did gain James's interest though when Susan took Candy by the hand to one of the bedrooms, and locked the door behind them. It looked like they made love rather than just have sex, as it was far more gentle at first, but eventually more intense than what James had witnessed with all the others. James resolved to keep Candy's identity hidden, she was beautiful he now saw, but Susan would have a lot of explaining to do with her husband when he saw this.

James felt exhausted just watching, but they just carried on. People were jumping in both pools, romping on the billiard table, women screwing men with dildo's, men sharing women, an orgy going on in the drawing room.

When Susan and Candy came back downstairs with very happy smiles, they joined the revelers in the outdoor pool after removing their clothes in the changing area. After a long kiss with their hands getting intimate, they jumped into the pool for sex with the other swimmers.

To James, it seemed to go on forever before anyone made motions to leave, and even then there were still sexual antics going on. He was very heavy lidded when the last car finally left and the limos picked up Susan and her staff.

Checking all the camera feeds, no one was left in or around the house although a good few lights had been left on. James was desperate to sleep, but he thought that if he retrieved his cameras now, he wouldn't have to worry about someone showing up early in the morning to clear up. He climbed into the front of the truck and headed over.

Counting the cameras as he collected them and putting them into his large bag, the smell of booze and sex was everywhere, and plastic glasses, toys and used condoms littered the floors. There were also pieces of fruit crushed into the floors, and tubs of ice cream. James had enjoyed watching the ice cream and fruit being used, in ways he'd never imagined, guiltily, as he imagined doing it with Alice.

Having got all of his cameras, James took a sandwich from the fridge and a bottle of wine back to the car park. He'd eaten all of his food and was hungry again. Once back at the car park, he took the last two cameras from the entrance, and after checking the monitor to make sure no one had come around while he'd been gone, he turned it off. He ate his sandwich, emptied the pee bottle, took a good drink of wine, and slept.

By the time he woke up, there were several other cars around him so he relieved himself in the bottle before driving away.

He dumped the bottle in a large industrial trash can by a gas station, where he also freshened up and got some coffee and a bagel, before continuing on his way.

Back at the hotel, he packed up the equipment he wanted to keep, and after shaving and showering, ate in the hotel cafe. He then took the truck, dumped the equipment he didn't want, and returned the truck to the rental company.

After spending the night in the hotel, he flew home the following morning, putting together the beginning of the movie that didn't contain any sex as he travelled, mindful of prying eyes on his screen.

CHAPTER 32

James was so glad to be home, unscathed, and he was especially delighted that it was also another Sunday and another roast lunch with Alice's family.

Alice hadn't taken James to the airport when he left, he'd gotten a cab, but she picked him up and took him home. She'd missed him as much as he'd missed her, and she was thrilled when he took her straight to his bed. She even told him that he should go away more often.

Lunch at Alice's parents had been just as good as before. This time her mother had made roast lamb with a redcurrant jelly which James really enjoyed. Tina and Bill were excited about being able to help with the website and offering their advice. They showed James some of the messages they'd responded to, and he couldn't fault them for their replies.

Alice's father wanted to know why she was glowing so much, and he was nonplussed when everyone started laughing.

James went home with Alice and stayed there for a couple of days. Not wanting to go home, he bought himself some clothing from a nearby store, along with some bathroom supplies. Alice didn't mind at all, she liked him being around and waiting for her when she got home. She even gave him a key, which surprised her greatly, but it felt the most natural thing to do.

When James finally went home to finish his movie, it took him three days to put it all together. It was a mix mash of photos in the beginning, with the prominent folk and their cars. It then moved to their arrival at the car park and then at the house, the costumes they wore, and the goings on in the house. The bathroom shots turned out great. Nearly everybody took off their masks to wash up, to take drugs, and it was a crucial element to the movie.

James was also moving Susan's assets around. He thought it would be apt if she could help finance the bullying site. Once the movie was finished and he had it on YouTube, he sent a press release to the New York Newspapers asking if they knew the people on his list, and giving them the link to the movie.

The news was massive on the East Coast. All involved were named, and although it wasn't illegal, apart from the drugs that were used, it was extremely embarrassing and shaming to them. Not to mention Susan. James had told the media who the organizer was and where she could be found.

Susan felt she was being hounded by everyone. Her phone kept ringing, her photo was being taken, voice recorders were being thrust into her face as questions were being asked, and reporters wanted her to speak into the many television cameras.

Her husband told her not to come home and that he was speaking to his lawyers, he wanted a divorce and to have custody of their children. She would have to fight in the courts to retrieve them, and she was barred from seeing them unless she was supervised. He would send her belongings to wherever she liked, but not to try to return to their house.

Susan was devastated. She couldn't fathom what the hell had happened. She watched the movie on YouTube and could barely comprehend that what she saw, was what happened at the party. She hadn't seen any cameras. The only person she could think of that would have been able to have set them up was her driver, and he totally denied it, which she believed. Which left someone from the S & M club. *Who on earth in the club wanted to ruin her and the other members? Was someone betrayed, and she just got caught up in it?*

That must be it, Susan thought, *a stupid jealous partner.*

Clients were calling and accused her of betraying them, selling them out, and that they would never return to her club or use her services ever again. Susan pleaded with them, telling them she'd been set up as well, but it was to no avail. The club was being avoided by the customers, Susan had to lay off her staff, and the only visitors were the curious who stood outside.

Then all her personal money left her. Everything she had. She still had her credit cards from the family account, but all the money she had accrued herself, her investments, everything, just went.

All that was dear to her, children, family, social standing, friends, money, club, lifestyle, all gone in one fell swoop. She felt totally and utterly, violated.

James didn't know all of this but he'd set it in motion so he could guess. After he'd heard Alice tell her story, the only thing he'd wanted to do was to hurt Susan in a way that would be somehow comparable to what she'd done to Alice. He didn't want to physically hurt her, or to send her to prison, or harm her family. Prison may have worked, but James had thought long and hard about it.

What he'd been encouraging with his website, the public humiliation, he'd put to the test and he liked it. Really liked.

Now he just had to fathom what to do with his father.

CHAPTER 33

James couldn't even remember the last time he'd seen his dad. He thought it was at his mom's funeral, but even then his dad didn't speak to him, or even offer to pay any of the costs. He'd just left it to James to deal with, then showed up like somebody who had a right to.

James had kept track of his dad, from a distance, but he had no love for him or even any respect left. He was still his only son, yet his dad had not even attempted to contact him after he left home. James still couldn't understand why, or when he did come across him at his mom's insistence, why his dad seemed so ashamed of him.

Joseph Wrigley, James's father, lived now in San Mateo, the next town over from Redwood City. He was still married to his second wife, and his two girls were both in high school.

James was very reluctant to meet his dad again, but he needed to eventually, if only to confirm that he was still as he remembered him.

Alice thought James should visit his demons as well, and James opening up to her only made her feel closer to him. She was aware that him talking about his father was hard, she couldn't imagine her own father abandoning her and ignoring her, but James needed to find peace, and accept him for whoever and whatever he was.

James watched him from a distance for many days. As he observed, he slowly realized that he had nothing left for his father apart from disdain.

As Joseph went about his business, James tried hard to recall a good memory of him but there was nothing there. It was almost as if he'd been just a daily visitor to the house rather than being his dad, and James thought that maybe he couldn't remember his dad playing with him, because it was when he was too young to recall it.

James could only really remember his father as someone who was usually gone when he got up, and when he came home he just kept to himself. Even at the weekends it was no different. Mom never had to work weekends then, and she and James would play and do stuff together, but James couldn't remember his dad ever being there. They would either leave him at home, or he would go out by himself.

Once he'd left, if he had to come by he would look at James with something like contempt, and if James had his customary bruises, he would tell him to defend himself and not just be a pathetic wimp.

The time when he left was the worst. Mom was a wreck and crying all the time. Then she had to work weekends, James lost his time with her, and it was a very bad time.

Joseph and his new family lived in a modest house, two levels with a single car garage. The roof was shingle and looked like it needed replacing, the red brick was old, and the window frames needed a lick of paint. The front door was in the center of the house with a bare front porch, and the grass was a little sparse, brown, but had been cut. A wooden six foot gate at the side of the garage led to the back yard, but there was no fence at the front and the neighborhood seemed safe. Just very old in its appearance.

James had no inclination to go inside, just as he had no interest at all in delving into his father's bank accounts or whatever else he kept on his computer.

Now that he was thinking about his father, he also got to thinking about his grandparents on that side of his family, and an aunt and uncle. He couldn't remember ever meeting them, but he knew they existed, although he'd made no effort to find them. His mom had told him that they had never wanted anything to do with them and they didn't even attend their wedding. James by then didn't care. He'd had enough of trying to make people like him, and so if his family were the same way, then he wasn't bothered.

James's mom was an only child, and her parents had been killed in a multi car crash before she got married.

Joseph wasn't as trim as James remembered, and he was still plain looking. His stomach had a paunch nowadays, his brown hair had receded a little, his only redeeming feature being the blue eyes that he'd given James. He wore glasses now.

Joseph's wife, Nicole, was an attractive woman, and James wondered how his father had attracted her. She was blonde who liked to wear it in a bun, buxom, a little overweight but only a tad, and her smile displayed her dimpled cheeks. She worked at Sears in customer service, held herself in a good posture, and her legs were well formed. She drove a Honda Civic, he a Toyota Carola, and neither car was very new.

Their two girls had turned out very prettily. Both attended the nearby San Mateo High School, the oldest Eleanor, was now sixteen, and her sister Kelly, was fourteen.

Like her mother, Eleanor was blonde haired that was long and straight, with some of her father's facial features, while Kelly had the same color hair as her father, but her mother's looks. Both were slim, and they seemed to be good kids.

None of the family seemed to do anything out of the ordinary. The girls liked to hang out with their friends in Hillside Mall, their Mom shopped for groceries in Safeway, and their Dad just seemed to go to work, then go home.

A couple of nights a week they would dine out together, nothing fancy, and the girls would also sometimes go to the movies, together, or with their various friends.

James was being very careful as he watched. He didn't do it every day, and when he did he would walk sometimes, wear different hats, and just try to avoid being spotted.

His father though, did go out alone one night, on a Wednesday. James hadn't stuck around the previous week, he'd assumed that it would be like the other nights, so once everyone was home he'd left to go to Alice's.

This particular night, he'd only hung around because Alice had said that she would be late. James wondered what excuse his father gave, or maybe it was all innocent and he was just running to the store for something.

James followed at a very safe distance, concentrating on his father's car so as not to miss him making a sudden turn.

When he turned into a housing neighborhood, it was obvious he wasn't shopping for anything, but maybe he was visiting a relative or a friend. The area looked familiar to James, he felt he'd been here before, but seeing his father parking outside a house, he took a quick turn onto another street and drove around the block, driving back past the house that his father was just entering.

James parked down the street and tried for almost an hour to recall why this neighborhood seemed familiar. He wondered if it was somewhere he used to come to when he was a boy, or if something occurred around here that had just stuck in his memory.

When it hit him, it was more with disappointment than with anything else.

His father had come to this address during a work day, and James had assumed it was just another insurance assessment. Maybe it was, but James needed to know now.

He moved his car closer, by an empty house that would give him a good view of the house that his father was inside. It was just a one level ranch home with a dark green mini parked outside the garage.

There was nothing to be seen through the windows at the front, James didn't want to start creeping around, so he stayed where he was. He left a message for Alice that he'd been held up in a meeting, but that he would still go over and let himself in. He hoped it wouldn't be too long, but he just needed to get something settled.

James didn't keep time, but he knew it had been at least an hour before the front door gently crept open.

He didn't have one of his night vision cameras or binoculars with him, so he filmed with his telephone that at least had a zoom feature, and he watched on the screen.

A short haired brunette had opened the door, but James could only see her profile. She looked very slim, although it was hard to determine as she was wearing a bathrobe. He began to think that maybe it was just a work follow up as his father stepped out the door, but then he arched back to kiss her, on the lips, that lingered for way too long. He was having an affair.

James didn't follow him home, he went straight to Alice's and had a late dinner with her. In a way, what James had witnessed only vindicated his mother, in that it wasn't her fault her husband had strayed. James acknowledged that his step mother was prettier than his mother, so if his father cheated on her, then he was probably a serial cheater.

It was just another sad situation.

CHAPTER 34

James's website was getting very popular. He was finding more organizations to refer the visitors to, and he was getting enquiries from companies who wanted to advertise.

This was good, but he only wanted advertisers if they were excellent employers. James stressed to them that he would make enquiries, and if he was to find that they advocated any kind of undue employee pressure, or didn't act fairly with them, then he would make it public and drop them immediately. He lost a few potential advertisers by doing it, but he felt it was well worth it.

Even with all the links, they were still getting emails, but Bill and Tina were handling them with increasing expertise. They really enjoyed doing it as well.

James did get a personal message from the boy in Florida, who was now a very happy pupil in a special school, and the kids who had bullied him had all been expelled. The Principal had been moved out, and his old school now had a no tolerance policy. He didn't miss going there, but was glad that the other children wouldn't have to suffer as he did.

James went back to the house that his father visited, and got a good shot of the woman he saw him kissing. It turned out she was slim, much younger than his father, good looking, and a yoga instructor.

He couldn't fathom what on earth she saw in his father, but she was seeing someone else who was more her age and quite a handsome guy. As James was still avoiding going into his father's business, he figured that the woman may have put in for an insurance claim and this was his father's fee for approving it. It made sense, he couldn't think of any other reason, or maybe his father just had a magnetism about him that James couldn't see.

James pulled a couple of stills from his phone that turned out better than expected, with good shots of his father exiting the house and kissing the woman. He still wondered what the attraction was for her.

One of the regular places that Joseph and his family went to for a meal was called Osteria Coppa, an Italian restaurant in San Mateo. A very good restaurant that not only makes its own pastas, they also use local organic products and the freshest ingredients. Its all glass storefront in the heart of the city makes for a very open ambience, and it is always busy.

On a night off from Alice, James dined there one night and vowed to return with Alice sometime. The food was delicious and he really liked the place.

He was just having a coffee and had asked for his bill when Joseph and his three girls came in.

James watched closely as they checked in, he couldn't hear them, and they were shown to their table. They didn't garner any other attention, they were just casually dressed, but a couple of young boys with their parents gave the two girls a good look. The girls noticed and giggled between them, as the host sat them down.

James sipped his coffee and put a credit card on the bill, still watching his father and step family as they were brought drinks, then some garlic bread and anti-pasta after they had ordered.

James's server came back with his card and receipt to sign, and James left a good tip as he pocketed the card and finished his coffee.

Getting up from the table, he walked slowly over to his father's table, they were all chatting, and standing at the edge of the table he interrupted and said,

"Hello dad, would you like to introduce me?"

It was like someone had slapped the four of them on the face at the same time, they just sat there open mouthed, staring at him.

"Well dad?" James asked. "Surely you'd like for me to finally meet my sisters." James smiled at the two girls who gaped up at him.

"Is this a joke?" stuttered Joseph, "who the hell are you?"

James looked at his red faced father who had a look of panic in his eyes as he looked at his son, his very different looking son.

"Come on dad, you know who I am. I'm the son you abandoned to start your new family, you know, the son you never contact or speak to. Would you like me to introduce myself to your wife and daughters?"

"You need to leave right now." His father didn't get up from the table but he frantically waved over their server, telling him "this man is pestering us, will you show him the way out please, he's causing a scene."

James had a handful of purposely made business cards in his hand, with his name and telephone number on, and he gently threw them over the table, hoping one of his sisters would secrete one and give him a call sometime.

"It's okay dad, I'm going. I don't know why you never liked me or why you deny my existence, but that's okay, I'm used to it now. Very pleased to meet you finally, Nicole, Eleanor, and Kelly," James smiled at each as he mentioned their name, "I hope we have chance to meet again."

"You stay away from my family" admonished Joseph, as James walked away, wishing he could return as a fly to hear the explanation from his father.

It was almost a week later before James got a call, he didn't think it was going to happen, but the oldest girl, Eleanor, was on the line.

"Are you really my brother?" She asked shyly.

"Yes, I am. Has your father told you the truth yet?"

"He says it's all a prank by one of his friends. How do I know you're telling the truth?" She asked.

"I think you suspect it's true, otherwise you would never have called me." James answered.

There was a long pause.

"You don't even have the same last name," she stated.

"I changed it to mom's after she died. Listen Eleanor, I know this is hard to believe, but you can look all this up on the computer. You may have done it already. I just thought the time was right for you and your sister to know that you have a brother. If you don't want anything to do with me, that's fine, I'll stay away."

"If you are our brother, what do you want from us?" Eleanor asked.

"Absolutely nothing apart from getting to know you a little. All of my mom's relatives died before I was even born, so you're all I have now. Do some research on the computer. I could give you all the details but you'll believe it more if you do it yourself."

"Why doesn't dad like you? Are you a bad person? Have you been in prison?"

"I have no idea why he doesn't like me Eleanor, but he never has. I'm not a bad person, and I haven't been to prison either. I promise."

"Can I call you back?" Asked Eleanor, hopefully.

"Anytime."

"Okay then, I will. Bye." Eleanor put the phone down and James really wanted to call her right back.

It was another long week for James before Eleanor called him back, and she and her sister wanted to meet him somewhere.

James suggested the mall as it was open, safe, and in public. That way, if they were ever questioned about it, they wouldn't get into as much trouble as they would if they came to his apartment.

Eleanor agreed and James met them both on a Saturday in the mall, buying them frozen yoghurts as he had a coffee.

Eleanor and Kelly had obviously done their homework, as they now accepted James as their step brother, although none of them mentioned the step part. It seemed it was still tense at home, their parents were barely talking, and the girls were keeping out of the way. They hadn't told either of the parents they were meeting James, and they asked him to promise not to tell. James did so.

Then it was like a thousand questions. What he did, what car did he drive, where did he live, was he married? As much as James was asked, he responded with his own questions. How was school, what grades did they get, what did they do for fun, did they have boyfriends?

The time passed very quickly and James was sorry when they said they had to go. He would have offered them a ride, but thought it not prudent at this time.

James told Alice about his sisters, she was shocked to learn he'd met them, and he told her how it came about in the restaurant, and his father's response. She couldn't understand why he continued to reject James, but she was happy that Eleanor had called him and that they'd all met.

James asked her if she would go with him the next time they met, he wanted her to meet them and vice versa, and Alice readily agreed. She was worried about what would happen if the girls father heard about it, especially to the girls, and James concurred. He certainly wasn't going to tell Alice he'd been spying on his father.

James and Alice met up with the two girls at the weekend, in the same place as James had met them before.

Again, it was a mass of questions. Is this your girlfriend, do you live together, is school tough, what movies do you like, are you good at math, how did you become a doctor, do you think we're good looking, how much money do you have, which hospital do you work at?

It seemed home life had quietened down for the two girls, it was almost back to normal which was very boring to them.

James asked them if they knew their grandparents and aunt and uncle.

"We know them but not very well," answered Eleanor, and she continued.

"They come over sometimes, usually together, but they never stay long. Dad talks to them alone for a while, they all start shouting about stuff, and then they leave.

They sent us birthday cards for a while and some presents, but then it stopped, and we haven't received anything since. They do call sometimes but it's only to talk to dad, they never talk to us or Mom.

It's weird. Our other grandparents are great, although dad isn't keen on them. We generally go over to their house with mom, and we meet up with our cousins and aunts and uncle.

Me and Kelly try not to get stuck in the middle. It was just a shock when you came along and said you were our brother."

James asked them if they knew where their father's relatives lived. They didn't, but they said they could easily find out, but wanted to know why.

James replied that he just wanted to get to the bottom of it all. It didn't matter if they wanted nothing more to do with anyone, he just needed to know.

The girls said they would get the addresses and let him know.

When it was time for them to go home, James and Alice gave them a ride and dropped them off around the corner from their house, everyone exchanging hugs.

Alice had really enjoyed meeting them, and she thanked James for including her.

In response, he asked her if she would go with him when he faced up to his grandparents, as he might need some moral support if they were going to be unfriendly.

Alice gripped his hand and replied, "We're in this together honey, good and bad. So where are we going for dinner tonight?"

CHAPTER 35

A new trend to James, although it had been around for a while, was cyber bullying. In many ways it was even worse in James's opinion, as it broadcast the sufferer's pain to potentially millions. It hadn't really caught on when James was in school, which he was thankful for as it was nasty.

There was help available, and Bill and Tina had been gallantly sending the victims there, but there was one case that they asked James to help with as they thought it was a dire situation.

It concerned a disabled girl, who'd fought her way from a wheelchair to walking with canes, but it still forced her to drag her right leg behind her. For some reason, this had raised the ire of a group of cheerleaders who were seemingly hell bent on forcing the girl out of their school.

It was hard to determine why. The girl, Jennifer Wood, wasn't popular with the guys, she wasn't a genius, and she didn't tell tales to the teachers. She was just someone who was trying to make the most of her situation, and be as normal as she could be.

Jennifer had sent a sampling of some of the texts she received on a daily basis, along with the link to the Facebook page that had been dedicated to her. It was awful.

Not only was she being called all kinds of names, such as retard, cock sucker, witch, cripple, ho, ugly, deformed, spastic, and a monster, there was other stuff as well. The cheerleaders awarded points to anyone who kicked her canes away to make her fall. More points were available for a push in the right location, or for good jokes about her disability. It was endless.

By far the worst thing, was the video that they'd posted on her page, as well as YouTube. They had staged a dance to the Thriller soundtrack, with the girls made up to resemble Jennifer in a zombie way, and they mimicked her walk with imaginary canes and the dragging of the leg.

Jennifer rightfully felt hated, unloved, alone, dumb, ugly, and quite suicidal. After what she'd been through just to get on her feet, she now felt like it had been a total waste of her time and effort.

James called Jennifer and her parents, not giving his real name, to find out their circumstances, more about Jennifer's plight, and what would be their perfect solution.

They were a very modest family who had little money. Everything they had was almost exclusively spent on Jennifer, as she still needed medication, treatment, and help.

They couldn't understand what they'd done, but they didn't want Jennifer to suffer anymore. They just didn't have the money, or the social standing, to do anything.

When James spoke privately with Jennifer, he told her of all the help centers that were available, but asked her what she herself really wanted.

Jennifer was like her parents, she didn't want much, just to be left alone.

When James asked her if she wanted to move, or be in another school, she replied she was happy where she lived, her parents couldn't afford another school, and so she would have to put up with it. She did had a couple of friends in school, but they were shy of being in her company during school, because of the ramifications.

On being asked how she'd feel if James was able to turn the tables, but that it could well be obvious that she would be behind it, Jennifer thought for a couple of minutes before saying that it would be worth it, as she was desperate for it all to stop.

James asked Jennifer to call her friends and to find out as much as she could about her tormentors. Where they lived, where they hung out, who their boyfriends were, where they partied. Whatever she could find out, she was to send the information to the email address that James gave her, and that although he would come to her town, he wouldn't meet her. Whatever happened, Jennifer had to keep it all confidential. James wanted to help her, but would walk away if she started talking to anyone. Including her parents.

Jennifer lived in a suburb of Dallas, Texas. James had a couple of days free so he flew down there once Jennifer sent him the information, which she was very quick to find. James guessed it was her desperation.

After hiring a car and booking into a hotel, James cruised around getting his bearings. He didn't like what he was going to do, it was dangerous, totally illegal, but talking to Jennifer he'd heard her cries. He felt sure she would overdose or something. Despite his relationship with Alice, James had to help.

Like her tormentors, Jennifer was sixteen now, but unlike them she had to take a special bus to school. The cheerleaders all had their own vehicles.

Jennifer wasn't bad looking but she had neglected herself. Didn't wear any make up or dress well, she just looked like a poor disabled girl. Her brown shoulder length hair was uncared for, her face pleasant, but needed her best features emphasized. She wasn't overweight or too thin, but again, her clothing did nothing for her.

One of the cheerleader's had a much older boyfriend who had his own house. He was the son of wealthy parents who indulged him, and he didn't seem to care that he was no doubt committing rape with his sixteen year old girlfriend. Not that she looked it, but that was the law.

Jennifer had been able to find out that the kids used the house at weekends to party. The boyfriend supplied the booze, but they never invited any other kids from school, as they didn't want to attract unwanted attention by having big parties. It was just the cheerleading group and their boyfriends. It was a neat setup that no one inside the group wanted to ruin.

James donned a disguise of blonde hair, glasses, and padding inside his mouth, before he bought some cameras from a spy shop in Dallas with cash. He was going to use similar equipment as he'd used on the cop in Redwood City, he just needed more cameras and he wouldn't be retrieving them. He normally liked to be tidy and clean up after himself, but he thought that with this one, it might be helpful for them to think that someone local had done it. One of their own. Keep them guessing and looking over their shoulders at each other with distrust.

The boyfriend's house posed a challenge for James as he would have to park near to the limit of the cameras range. The large house had no near neighbors yet, there was construction going on, but even the builder's cabin wasn't within range.

It was so flat around the house, the only location he could see that might do was behind a couple of trees. It was risky, but there was nothing else. If questioned, he would just have to pretend he was sleeping off a few drinks, and didn't realize the dirt track by the trees was private property.

The house itself was very impressive considering the young man who lived in it did nothing. James thought he maybe was like himself, just younger, more intelligent, and got richer quicker. It was highly doubtful, but he gave it a thought.

James pretended to look around the vacant lots as he waited for the occupant of the house to leave. There was nothing close by that he could just make a quick trip to, it was miles to anything of any significance.

The builders weren't sales reps so they didn't bother him, and there was no model house available yet. Even when the land would be taken, the boyfriend's house was set well back and away from the other lots, so unless he set up a commercial sound system suitable for a rock band, his future neighbors wouldn't be calling the police for excessive noise.

Just as James was beginning to wilt in the heat of Texas, and thinking the young man was going to stay home, his triple doored garage opened and he drove out in one of his cars, a silver Porsche 911. James got a glimpse of him, and he looked a handsome guy with thick wavy black hair, framing a narrow face that was partially hidden by the aviator sunglasses. James was wearing sunglasses also. It was too bright and glaring not to.

Watching him leave, James returned to his car and drove to the house, the builders not paying any attention to him.

The house was a mixture of stone, and sand colored brick, two levels, with a high pillared entrance. The property itself was enclosed by a low wrought iron fence at the front, which turned into a high, white wooden looking fence around the rear, and the entrance gate in iron was open. Beyond the gate it was just gravel for the whole width of the house, the grass at the sides surprisingly green in the high temperatures.

James wasted no time in admiring the house or entering it, along with his bag of goodies. Inside it was all open on the first floor, apart from the doors into the two bedrooms. One was obviously the master, with its size and personal belongings, and it was at the side of the very high ceilinged family room. It was a very masculine house, big screen TV's, leather couches and armchairs, sporting paraphernalia on the walls, and a pool table and a bar on one side of the house. No flowers, few picture frames, more practical than decorative.

The hardwood floors were broken up in places by good quality rugs, that added a little color to the home.

Up the grand staircase there were three more bedrooms and bathrooms, but they looked very basic and not that welcoming.

All the bedrooms were fully carpeted, but the ones upstairs didn't feel as soft as they did on the first floor, nor were the towels as thick. All the rooms upstairs overlooked the family room, with a balcony around it to enter the individual rooms.

As he went around the house that had been left unarmed, James placed his tiny cameras in all the places he thought would be used by the young visitors. It was a man's house, and it was clean and organized. No doubt a housekeeper came in, and probably a lawn care crew as well, along with pool maintenance.

The pool was large and you looked out on it from the family room and the adjoining breakfast table. It looked very welcoming with it's fountain facing the house, and the Jacuzzi at the side.

James peeped into the adjoining garage before leaving, and admired the Harley Davidson and the new Range Rover before letting himself out and locking the door behind him.

He then drove down to the dirt track that he'd seen earlier, parked behind the trees after turning the car around, and checked the cameras. They were far from perfect but they would do. Whatever he got on film he would edit, and as long as it would identify the cheerleaders, which they would, then they would suffice. It was mainly the positioning that disappointed him, but there were few hiding places in the house.

When James returned to his hotel, he asked the concierge if he could recommend anyone to do a make over for a young girl. The concierge thought he knew someone who would be perfect, and that he would call James's room when he located her number and availability.

James also asked him for the name and number of a VW dealership with a good reputation, and he took that number up to his room.

After ordering room service, James called the car dealer and asked to speak to an available sales person.

Room service knocked on the door minutes after he finished his call, and after he wheeled the cart in and James gave him a tip before he left, the room phone rang. It was the concierge and James wrote down the information, thanking him for his service.

James ate heartily. Being in Texas he had to have a steak, and the hotel provided a very juicy and delicious one. Despite its size, James polished it off, along with the baked potato, mushrooms, onions, and asparagus, washing it down with a fine claret.

Opening his laptop after pushing the cart out of the door into the corridor, James sent Jennifer an email, which she replied to within seconds. The one thing that James knew only too well, was that if you're lonely, and don't have much of a life, then a new email was exciting.

Jennifer had heard that the cheerleading group were going to the house the following night. She only knew that because someone had spoken about it in class and her friend had overheard. When James replied, thanking her for the information, he also told her that he was arranging a make over for her at the weekend, as a treat, and he also asked Jennifer if she could drive.

James had a broad grin as he waited for Jennifer to reply.

When she confirmed that she could and had her license, James told her of the VW dealership and that she had an appointment there on Saturday morning at 10am. She was to pick out any vehicle she wished, it was all taken care of, and he congratulated her on her new car. He would arrange her make over for the following day, Sunday, and he would drop her another line with the details.

Sending the email, James was still smiling from ear to ear as he imagined her delight, and he picked up the phone to call the lady who would transform Jennifer's appearance.

Once he confirmed that she would be available on Sunday, James told her that he needed her to not only take Jennifer to a beauty salon, but to also change her whole wardrobe. He would wire the money directly to her account to cover her fees and the services, and when she suggested a price, he added another five thousand to it. He got her bank account number, then gave her Jennifer's address and email address, so she could touch base with her.

James sent Jennifer another email telling her to expect another message, loving the excitement in her reply.

His business done for the evening, James poured himself another glass of wine and called Alice.

The following day, James investigated the private schools that were well within Jennifer's range with a new car. Speaking to the principals, he explained Jennifer's situation, her current grades, her age, but most importantly her fragility. Finding two schools that he thought would be perfect and that would welcome her mid-term, he sent the links for the schools to her mother's email address, asking her to talk it over with her husband and Jennifer. The school fees were of no consequence. They would be paid if Jennifer wanted to go.

After James had a good lunch in the hotel restaurant, he made his way to the hiding place by the boyfriend's house after calling in to a deli for a sandwich, chips, and some bottled water. The builders had already left when he arrived, so after setting up his laptop with the camera feeds, and seeing no one inside the house, he took a nap lying in the shade of one of the trees.

By the time James woke up, surprised by how long he'd been out but feeling refreshed, the boyfriend was home and putting twelve packs of beer in the kitchen fridge. There were a couple of cameras with audio, and he heard the rap music that he was playing, having no idea who the artist was.

Not all the cheerleaders were in this clique group, but they probably complied with the rules to stay in their coveted roles. The ringleader wasn't the oldest girl, but she no doubt attained it with having this place to go to, with booze freely available.

As James watched the kids slowly arrive, he wondered what they told their parents they were doing.

None of them were dressed up, it was just the usual teenager attire of jeans, shorts, baggy pants, tee shirts, and flip flops. The girls were attractive and slim, and the boys tried to look cool with their uncombed hair and ill fitting clothes.

The ringleader was the pick of the girls, a long haired blonde in ripped jeans, a cropped top showing her midriff, and on arrival she kissed her boyfriend and hung on his neck. Not minding his hand stroking her bare back. The boyfriend was leaning back against the bar and he had a beer in his other hand, and as the others arrived they helped themselves to whatever drinks they wanted. One of the other girls, a long haired brunette, handed a beer to the ringleader, and everyone lounged around, talking trash about people that James didn't know, but that he recorded for Jennifer. There was no mention of her, but they were calling others assholes, or perverts, and such like.

It was all fairly boring to James, but once they'd had a few drinks it began to liven up, especially when one of the boys produced some joints and they all took some draws. They then hit the hard liquor, the music got louder, and the couples started dancing and making out.

James ate his sandwich and drank some water. He really wanted to turn the car engine on for the a/c as it was still unbearably hot, and he wished he'd brought a cooler to keep the water cold. Even bottled water tastes like crap when its warm.

By the time it was midnight, most of them looked worse for wear and they began to move to the bedrooms, apart from one couple who looked liked they'd passed out on one of the couches.

As James watched, it was obvious they were all sexually active and had been for some time, there were no inhibitions with any of them. They were no sooner in the bedrooms when all their clothes were off, and they were pleasuring each other. The ringleader did a striptease for her guy like a professional, so much so he almost expected the guy to slip dollar notes into her tiny black g string.

Once they started to fall asleep, mostly naked on top of the beds, James closed up his laptop and relieved himself against one of the trees before slipping away. He didn't put his lights on until he hit the paved street, and he drove at the speed limit so as not to attract attention. The evening had been very enlightening, although very uncomfortable in what he'd witnessed.

James flew out the following day, glad to be going home, but really happy about what he'd been able to do for Jennifer.

He was in the airport when he got a text on his prepaid phone. Jennifer had picked out her car, and the salesperson needed the money wired. James was grinning as he had it wired, seeing the picture in his mind as Jennifer first had to wait, and then was given, the keys to her brand new Beetle.

Once James was home, he had time before going over to Alice's, to put a short movie together of the trash talk, the drinking, weed smoking, the sex, from the previous evening. He didn't post it on the social media sites. Instead, he sent it as an MP3 file to Jennifer, along with a note.

Dear Jennifer, You are no doubt enjoying your new car and you will have another fun day tomorrow. Your parents may also have told you that you have the opportunity to go to another school. I hope you do so, they will give you a better education which will behove you when you're older. There are two schools to choose from, both know of your disability, they have great reputations, and they have zero tolerance for bullies. I hope you will give both serious consideration and that you choose one of them.

You may be wondering why I'm doing this for you. I don't, and can't, do this for everybody. It would be great if I could, but it's not possible. You hit a nerve Jennifer, and I was able to help. I too was vilified during my school years, and at times I felt suicidal. Practically all the time I was in school I was depressed, and I'm still not sure how I survived it. I wasn't disabled and I can't imagine how much more difficult that has been for you.

I have enclosed a file for you that you are free to use as you wish. I am destroying what I have, so this is yours, and solely yours.

It's not for me to advise you how to use this file. I myself have had issues which I've sought to rectify, and still have some, but what I feel I had to do for my own contentment doesn't apply to you.

You have to decide for yourself what you need to do. I have given you the tool, you will know in your heart how to use it, or even if you need to. It's entirely up to you.

It has been my greatest pleasure to have been able to do something for you, and I hope to receive updates from you at regular intervals.

Your friend.

When Jennifer went back to school, making everyone almost choke with her new car, new look, and new clothes, she was really looking forward to receiving a new text message. It didn't take long. As usual, it was similar to what they always were, in that she was a ho, her rates had no doubt gone up to pay for her new look and car, but she was still a retard.

Jennifer replied that this was her last week at this crummy school, but if she wasn't left alone and the Facebook page discontinued, then she would have no choice but to post a video she had obtained. Jennifer attached a clip from the video, laughing quietly as she pressed 'enter.'

Jennifer wrote to James telling him about her fantastic weekend, and that she was looking forward to starting at her new school. She also told him how she replied to the text, and that since sending her reply she had received no others. The Facebook page had been removed, and although she was getting filthy looks, she enjoyed them.

James was very proud of her. He wired the money for two years at the new school, to take her to graduation. He also wired more money, to cover the cost of the school uniforms and for the books Jennifer would need, but also for some specialist medical treatment for her disability.

CHAPTER 36

James's sisters made good on their promise within a few days, and James and Alice took them to lunch before making their way to his grandparents house.

James was as nervous as he'd ever been, but whatever happened, he was in a good place now with Alice and his sisters.

He hadn't gotten in touch with his grandparents. He and Alice were just hoping to catch them at home, and if they were out, then James was going to leave them a note with his number, asking them to call. He hoped they were out.

They lived across the bay in Livermore, and using the GPS system in the car, they found their house that was in a bit of a maze.

It sat on the corner of the street and was just one level, but the steps leading up to the front door suggested that it probably had a basement. The front yard was well tended, the mature trees gave some good shade, and the wooden sided home looked like it was well maintained.

James and Alice weren't dressed up, but their casual clothing was smart, and they looked like a successful couple.

As they pulled up, Alice asked James if he was ready to do this, and after he nodded, she took his hand as they made their way up the steps to the front door.

After James pressed the doorbell, he felt his stomach churning as they waited for someone to answer.

A small woman with permed white hair answered the door, wearing a multicolored shapeless dress.

"Can I help you?" She asked politely, smelling a little of lavender.

"I'm James, and this is my girlfriend Alice. I know this will be a big surprise to you, but I'm the son of Joseph Wrigley."

The old woman looked at James for many seconds as she took this information on board, and then left them standing there as she went back into the house, but leaving the door open. They heard her shout, "Harold, you need to come to the front door."

James and Alice looked at each other and shrugged.

The old woman came back to the door then looked back as Harold came into view.

"Who is it Barbara? What do they want?" Asked the balding old man as he shuffled to the door with a cane.

"You'd better repeat what you said to me" Barbara told James.

"Hello Sir. My name is James, and I'm the son of Joseph Wrigley."

Harold stood with Barbara and looked at James for several seconds before replying.

"You mean our Joseph?"

"Yes sir. I'm your grandson, and this is my girlfriend Alice."

"Did Joseph send you here?" Asked Harold.

"No Sir. For some reason he has never liked me, and we don't have any kind of relationship. We came here today to ask you if you dislike me as well. If you do, I'll say sorry for disturbing you, and we'll go home."

"You sure Joseph didn't send you young man?" Asked Harold.

"He won't even talk to me Sir, he's barely said a word to me since he left me and my mom when I was still in school."

"Jeez. I think you'd both better come inside then. What was your name young lady?" Harold asked Alice.

Alice told him and they went inside, following the slow moving couple as they took them into the kitchen and instructed them to sit at the table, which they did.

Harold was thin and wiry while Barbara was plump. They were both on the short side, but with Harold it was probably because of age and his stance with the bent knees.

Barbara offered them some coffee or a soda, and both just asked for water.

When everyone was settled, Harold took the floor. It was quickly apparent to James and Alice that Harold liked to talk, and that he also did Barbara's talking as well.

"So, you're our James are you?" Asked Harold.

"Yes sir. But I don't have your last name anymore. I changed it to mom's."

"How is your mom James? It's been a long time since we last saw her."

178

James looked at Alice before replying.

"She was killed Sir, several years ago by a drunken driver. Didn't you know?"

Harold looked at Barbara this time, who looked sad and shocked.

"No, we didn't son I'm sorry to say," Harold continued, "I wish we had. Tell me, what do you know about your father?"

"Actually, not a lot. Mom missed him very much when he left us, but she never talked about him. Like I said before, he kind of disowned me, and even when I buried mom he never spoke to me. He came, then he left. He even denies I exist to his two daughters. I don't know what I did to him, but I have no feeling left toward him," James replied.

"And you think we're the same?" Asked Harold.

"That's what I came to find out."

"Oh Jeez. This is all my fault son, I'm sorry to say. I need to tell you a story, but it won't excuse us for not paying more attention to you. I can only imagine what you must think of us."

With no comment coming from James, Harold told his story.

"What I'm about to tell you will probably shock you, because if there is anything I know about Joseph, it is that he can keep things hidden. Well hidden.

Joseph is our oldest child, and when he was growing up we knew he was secretive, but it never really bothered us. We had a common family problem, in that money or things would keep disappearing, and everyone would blame each other. In hindsight, we should have done more to find out who was doing it, as we might have avoided what went on later.

Anyway, they all started growing up, and Joseph went off to college while his younger brother and sister were still in high school. We didn't see him that often when he went, he was on the East coast, but he would call sometimes. He usually asked for money, but he said he was doing well in his courses and so we sent what we could. That was our big mistake. We had no inkling, but Joseph had dropped out of school and was spending most of his time in Atlantic City, gambling.

It was much later when we found out about it, well after he'd come home, gotten a job in Insurance, and said he was marrying your mother because she was pregnant with you. We tried talking him out of it, but his mind was set, and before we knew it, they were married, and we hadn't even been invited. We felt shunned, but Joseph told us your mom didn't want any fuss as she was very shy.

I don't know why I continued to trust him, but then Joseph then talked us into buying the house you were raised in, along with all the land. We know now of course that there wasn't much land, or that we didn't buy the property, but at the time it looked like a huge deal. So much so, that we took out a loan on this house, and put our life savings into it as well. He did put some of that money into the house, but only as a down payment to keep the mortgage reasonable. He didn't buy it outright, or the land he'd shown us, instead he took the rest of the money to Vegas and gambled it away.

Joseph has this idea that he's a good gambler. He's a good liar, but he's no gambler. Sure, he wins sometimes and big, but then he usually loses it all back. We only found out about the gambling when we got a knock on the door from some nasty looking guys who had been trying to find him for years, from Atlantic City. Seems he left there without paying his tab, so I was forced to re-mortgage my house to prevent him from being hurt. They didn't say they were going to harm him, but they didn't look like they were going to call the police either. So I paid his debt.

Then I went to see your dad. Of course, he totally denied it all and said he had no money to repay me, so I told him to sell a part of the land. That's when I found out there was no land, or no house to sell.

I thought for sure your mother knew about all this, that she had conspired with Joseph, so we stopped visiting or asking you and your parents over. I think Joseph blames your birth for his problems, which is ridiculous, but I think he looks at you as bad luck. He gambles, so he's superstitious, but he conveniently forgets that he was losing money way before you came along.

The biggest problem for us was that with having no savings left, no assets, and now a mortgage to pay, we couldn't send Joseph's brother and sister to college. They could only go to the community one, and they had to work part time to give themselves some money to pay for their books. They rightly felt very aggrieved at the situation their older brother had put them in, and they still do. Mainly now because of what he did to Barbara and myself. With having a mortgage to pay again, we also had to go back to work, so we do pet and house sitting at various places.

Joseph as you know got married again. He never told us why he'd left you and your mom, but we would go over from time to time, all of us, to ask him to repay some of the money he owed us. When he would tell us he had nothing to give, the shouting would start, and we would end up leaving.

Joseph still gambles. He secretes money away from god knows where, probably insurance scams, and then goes off to Reno we believe, to gamble. He is sick, but he doesn't know it, and whenever we've suggested he gets help, he tells us to mind our own business.

We know now son that your mom wasn't a party to his gambling, just as his current wife isn't. She probably has no idea. But for the sake of the rest of our family, we have had to stay away from Joseph.

We don't dislike you son, but I can understand why you think that, but hell, we don't even know you. We have no excuse. We should still have sent you a birthday card or something, and to our regret we've wrongly punished you, and your step sisters, for something your father has done. This is all my fault. I'm a stubborn man and as the head of the family I prevented anyone from contacting you or your mother. Barbara kept asking me to give you a call or something, but I wouldn't, because I was stupid. We have all suffered from my idiocy, but you James have probably suffered the most. I can't believe that Joseph never told me that your mom was killed, and I really don't know how you coped with no family around you to help.

I just hope you'll forgive me in particular, and accept all of our utmost apologies."

By now, James was the only one without a tear in his eye. He had no idea his father gambled. If his grandparents knew that Joseph slept around as well, they weren't saying, but James didn't think they knew.

He held out his hand to Harold, "Of course I accept your apology."

Harold grasped James's hand with both of his, and then everyone hugged each other, warmly, with love, and many more tears and apologies.

The old couple then took them on a tour of their home, showing the pictures of James's relatives, their completed jig saw puzzles that they'd framed, explaining where all the little ornaments had come from.

James and Alice took them both out for an early dinner, half of which they took home with them for their following day's lunch. Alice talked about her job, how she'd met James, and James told his grandparents how he worked first at the locksmith's, and then at the IT company, making good investments, and about his new website.

The explanation for the website made his grandparents tear up again, but James and Alice told them those days were gone and they were moving on. They just wanted to help others in that situation.

On taking them home, James gave them his contact information as did Alice, and promised to see them again very soon. Maybe even with his sisters, which they thought was a great idea.

On their way home, Alice thought that the day was the best ever, and thanked James for asking her to go with him. When they went to sleep later, she cuddled into him and they both slept very peacefully.

CHAPTER 37

The following morning, James let Alice sleep in a little before taking her some coffee. They were going to go over to her parents again for lunch. James looked forward to it now virtually every week.

Alice invited James back into bed but he declined, telling her to put a sweater on as he wanted to taste some sea air before lunch.

She thought he was funny but obliged, quite liking the idea of feeling the breeze by the ocean. It was one of the best things of living near the coast to be able to do that, and like most people, she didn't think she did it often enough.

He took her back to Half Moon Bay, and they strolled the shore as the morning fog lifted, the sun warming them as they kept just out of reach of the lapping water. It was breezy, but it felt good, very refreshing to their senses.

Stopping to turn back, James said, "I'd like to have a couple of dogs, a cat, and maybe some of those tiny goats."

"Really?" Asked Alice, laughing, "You don't have much room in your apartment for them."

"Don't you like animals?" He was serious.

"You know I do James. What's brought this on?"

He took both her hands in his.

"I was just thinking that's all," he smiled. "I feel at peace finally, and I thought having a pet or two around would be really nice. You've made me a better man Alice. I was heading in the wrong direction. Meeting you again was the best thing that's ever happened to me."

"Thank you James, that means a lot to me, but I think it should be me thanking you."

"I need to tell you something Alice."

"Are you sick? Is there something wrong?" She responded, worried now.

James grinned at her, seeing the concern on her face.

"No, I'm fine. I'm in love with you Alice. Deeply in love." He sunk down onto his knees. "Will you do the honor of marrying me?"

Alice looked down at him, she knew she was crying but didn't care, and she knew she was in love with him too.

"Yes, yes, yes!"

She went to her knees and kissed him all over his face, hugging him in absolute delight.

Other beach goers looked at them, wondering what they were doing and why they were so happy.

Breaking off her hug for a moment, Alice asked James why he asked her about the animals.

"I just needed to know that when we get our own place, that you won't mind there being animals everywhere."

"Of course not, just as long as you won't mind our children being amongst them."

"Thank you Alice. You have made me so happy. C'mon, I know of a store that's open. Let's go and get you a ring before we have lunch."

"I'll race you to the car" She shouted back at him, as she'd already set off.

Alice knew the ring she wanted as soon as she saw it, but still looked at the others. When she put it on, it looked perfect on her finger, and it dazzled. James saw the look on her face as she admired it under the light, and he handed over his credit card to the saleslady, who wanted to know if they needed it boxed and wrapped.

"This is staying right where it is" declared Alice.

After leaving the store, Alice was almost skipping in delight, but they bought some wine and cold champagne on the way to her parents.

Alice kept her hand hidden in her jeans pocket as they let themselves into the unlocked house, the dog signaling their arrival with an excited cry. Her mom noticed the look on her daughter's face and immediately asked if everything was okay. Alice got her mom and dad together and told them she had something to show them, as James watched with amusement behind her. Her brother John wasn't in the least interested, as he watched football from his normal prone position.

With a quick look back at James, who nodded, Alice took her hand out of her pocket and fluttered her fingers in front of her parents. Her mom screamed in delight, and her dad hugged and kissed her, before going to James and hugging him.

"Do I have your permission then Bill? Asked James in Bill's death grip.

"You're damn right you do, and you might want to start calling me dad."

Tina then gave James a hug and a kiss as Bill went back to his daughter, giving her another hug and taking a closer look at her ring

"I don't think you got that in the dollar store" he commented, seeing the light reflect off the diamond.

"I don't suppose anyone would like a drink would they?" asked James, opening one of the bottles of champagne.

"I'll get some glasses" smiled Tina.

"Get one for John as well," added James.

John got up on hearing this, and congratulated his sister and James.

Bill wanted to make a toast once everyone got a glass, and they all stood in a circle.

"As a father, you wonder if this day will ever come and what you will say. But to see the happiness in your daughter's face, who is so dearly in love with a man you've liked since first meeting him, makes it very easy. Thank you for what you've done James, welcome to our family, and very many congratulations to you both."

It was quite an afternoon and evening.

Alice couldn't stop looking at the ring on her finger. She'd never thought of getting married, but now she was engaged, it was like a million different things were going through her mind.

Tina had cooked some Pheasant for lunch, which was a first for James but he really liked it. Everybody seemed to be asking questions. Casual wedding? Formal? Where will you live? Who do you want to invite? Maid of honor? Best man? Which church? Reception? Rehearsal dinner? Honeymoon? Kids? When?

Alice had no idea. She'd never got as far as dreaming what her wedding would entail, so she was very interested when James was asked his opinion.

"Well," he began, "I firmly believe that a wedding is more important to the bride than it is to the groom, so whatever Alice wants, that's what we'll do. No arguments. The only idea I have, is that we all go to Maui, we get married on the beach, and we all have a truly memorable vacation. I would pay for it, and we could all have a blast."

"What about your relatives James? You know your father would stop your sisters from attending our wedding," Alice warned.

"Oh I can take care of him, he's no problem. I'll deal with him this week."

"You think so?"

"I know so Alice."

"Well, if you're sure. Wouldn't it all cost a small fortune to go there? It sounds good to me, it's not like we can fill up a church with friends." She smiled.

"If Alice wants a big wedding here, we would still need to pay for it along with a honeymoon somewhere. It would probably cost as much to do that, as for all of us to go somewhere to be together, and yet be sometimes apart," James smiled at his bride to be. "I only have one friend, someone who used to keep me from harm, and I'm sure he would love to be my best man. Especially in Maui. The only other person I would want there would be the Locksmith, but since he retired I've lost track of him. Alice no doubt has a couple of friends in the hospital, but I can charter a flight easily enough with room for everyone. "

"If we went there, would I still be able to plan my daughter's big day?" asked Tina.

"I haven't looked into it, but I'm positive that you still have to plan everything around what the hotels offer."

"Let me check on the computer," offered John, who liked the prospect of a free vacation in Maui.

"I would want to contribute to my girl's wedding day. It's my responsibility you know." Bill stated.

"If this is something that Alice wants to do, then you can still contribute to the wedding." James told him, winking at Alice.

Bill cursed himself for opening his mouth as he thought about the cost of a wedding.

"You should take a look at these Sis, they look great" John said.

Alice sat down and looked at the websites her brother had found, liking the idea of getting married on the beach, as she looked at the pictures and the scenery.

"Mom. Why don't you take a look and do some comparisons. I can't decide or even think right now, I'm still enjoying this." She flashed her ring.

"Besides," she continued, smiling at James, "we have to find a house for all our animals to live in."

FOOTNOTE

Unfortunately, recent bullying statistics show that bullying is on the rise among young adults, teens and children. The rise in these bullying statistics is likely due to a fairly recent form of bullying seen in recent years called cyber bullying. This type of bullying has gotten immense media attention over the past few years, sighting instances of cyber bullying pushed too far, and in many cases leading to cases of teen suicide or death. Many bullying statistics and studies have found that physical assaults have been replaced with constant cyber assaults in the form of bashing, rumors and other hazing content, targeted at a single student or group of students.

Bullying statistics:

- About 42 percent of kids have been bullied while online with one in four being verbally attacked more than once.
- About 35 percent of kids have been threatened online.
- About 58 percent of kids and teens have reported that something mean has been said about them or to them online.

- Other bullying statistics show that about 77 percent of students have admitted to being the victim of one type of bullying or another.
- The American Justice Department bullying statistics, show that one out of ever 4 kids will be bullied sometime throughout their adolescence.
- 46 percent of males, followed by 26 percent of females, have admitted to being victims in physical fights, as reported in one report of bullying statistics by the Bureau of Justice School.

Other bullying facts:

- As these bullying statistics indicate, bullying is just getting worse in American schools. Many studies have shown that increasing domestic violence at home are leading to an increase in bullying online and at school.
- Researchers note that one way to help begin to lower these bullying statistics is to tell an adult when it is happening.
- According to the i-Safe American survey of students bullying statistics, about 58 percent of kids admit to never telling an adult when they've been the victim of a bullying attack.
- Another way to stay safe from bullies is to inform the school if the attacks are taking place on school property or have something to do with the school.

- Ignore messages sent by cyber bullies.

Based on the bullying statistics we found, it is clear that cyber bullying is on the rise more so than any other type of bullying. Many students report seeing these types of bullying in chat rooms, social networking websites like MySpace.com, and Facebook.com. There has also been websites dedicated to targeting a student or group of students. Many bullying studies revealed that students who are part of a minority group of students based on their gender, race, socioeconomic status as well as sexual preference, are reasons other students use to harass and cyber bully one another. Many of these students are forced to deal with at-school bullying and have it follow them home as they see hurtful comments and rumors being said about them throughout the Internet. While this isn't always a school-related issue, many schools are cutting down on this type of behavior from occurring at school, by limiting computer time and prohibiting many of the social websites used to spread the hurtful information.

Because of the wide-spread amount of bullying it is more important than ever for parents and teachers to check in with children about bullying. Many students might be afraid to tell an adult or parent, which is why parents and teachers need to be aware of the signs of bullying and to pay attention to what is going on with their child or student. Another one of the best ways to handle bullying, to help lower these numbers reported in bullying statistics, is open communication. Students and children should be encouraged to tell a trusted adult, parent or teacher about any kind of bullying attack. It is the best way to help stop the situation from getting worse, and to help prevent bullying from targeting more and more victims.

Sources: http://www.isafe.org

Workplace bullying on the rise, according to new study

By Debra Auerbach, CareerBuilder Writer

Most workers, even those who love their jobs, would probably say their job has caused them stress at some point. Throw in job insecurity, an increased workload and intensified pressure to perform, and stress levels can hit the roof. On top of that, some workers may also be faced with workplace bullying.

While workplace bullying isn't new, it is becoming more prevalent. According to a new CareerBuilder study, 35 percent of workers said they have felt bullied at work, up from 27 percent last year.

Bullying can cause more harm than hurt feelings or bruised egos; 17 percent of the workers who said they've felt bullied also reported that they quit their jobs to escape the situation. Sixteen percent said they suffered health problems as a result.

The profile of a bully

The study, which included more than 3,800 workers nationwide, revealed that bullies can be found at all levels within a company. Of workers who felt bullied, most pointed to incidents with their bosses (48 percent) or co-workers (45 percent). Thirty-one percent say they have been picked on by customers and 26 percent by someone higher up in the company other than their boss. Fifty-four percent of those bullied said they were tormented by someone older, while 29 percent said the bully was younger.

Words used as weapons

While bullying can <u>sometimes be physical</u>, words can also wound. Workers reported being bullied in the following ways:

- Falsely accused of mistakes -- 42 percent
- Ignored -- 39 percent
- Used different standards or policies toward me than other workers -- 36 percent
- Constantly criticized -- 33 percent
- Someone didn't perform certain duties, which hurt my work -- 31 percent
- Yelled at by boss in front of co-workers -- 28 percent
- Belittling comments were made about my work during meetings -- 24 percent
- Gossiped about -- 26 percent
- Someone stole credit for my work -- 19 percent

- Purposely excluded from projects or meetings -- 18 percent
- Picked on for personal attributes -- 15 percent

Speaking up

It takes courage to confront a bully or report the aggressor to human resources, but speaking up is often the only way to stop it.

Bullied workers have handled the situation in different ways:

- 49 percent of victims reported confronting the bully themselves.
- 50 percent of those who confronted the bully said the bullying stopped; 11 percent said it got worse; 38 percent said the bullying didn't change.
- 27 percent reported it to their HR department.
- 43 percent of those who reported it to HR said action was taken; 57 percent said nothing was done.

Rosemary Haefner, vice president of human resources at CareerBuilder, says, "Bullying can have a significant impact on both individual and company performance. It's important to cite specific incidents when addressing the situation with the bully or a company authority and keep focused on finding a resolution."

Three tips for taking action

Here are three ways to handle a workplace bullying situation:

1. **Keep a record. Write down all bullying incidents, documenting places, times, what happened and who was present.**
2. **Try talking it out. Consider talking to the bully, providing examples of how you thought you had been treated unfairly. It's possible the bully may not be aware that he is making you feel this way.**
3. **Focus on resolution. When sharing examples with the bully or a company authority, center the discussions on how to make the working situation better or how things could be handled differently.**

PREVIOUS PUBLICATIONS

STONEBRIDGE MANOR

PROSPECTS

UPCOMING RELEASE

THE INNOCENT CHILDREN

Made in the USA
Middletown, DE
05 June 2021